BURY ME

a novel

Dianna Dann

Wayward Cat Publishing

ISBN 978-1-938999-28-4
Library of Congress Control Number: 2016952237
Wayward Cat Publishing
Palm Bay, Florida
www.waywardcatpublishing.com
Cover art copyright © 2016 Wayward Cat Publishing
Photo of girl by ongap via istockphoto

BURY ME

Prologue

Hannah

It was just a refrigerator magnet—not meant to be noticed by anyone but me. Molded roughly out of some kind of clay, it was shaped like a cat perched and alert with its front paws together, its tail curled across them. One of those black and white tuxedos. Looks like he's dressed for a party. He's smiling. Silly, really.

I found it when I cleaned out my room before moving over to Orlando for college all those years ago. I'd turned everything else over to the police, but I guess this one little thing got lost in my mess. It was too late to return it then, so I put it on the refrigerator in the kitchen of my new place—to remind me of who I was and who I wanted to be. None of my roommates asked about it. Then I took it with me when I moved back home and put it on Mel's fridge. She said nothing.

It wasn't until this week, when I brought Meagan across the country to visit her Gram—she hadn't seen Mel since she was a baby—that it was finally noticed.

"It's a cat," she squealed and reached up for it.

Meagan's five now. Still too young to be told the truth of it. But I'll take the magnet back home with us. And one day, I'll tell her what it means to me.

Part One

Lenore

1.

I sometimes dream of my mother. She sits at the kitchen table, cocooned by stacks of folded, faded, yellowed newspapers. Her sharp elbows pounding the table top, her arms at odd angles, she's talking, talking. I can't hear what she's saying—a buzzing, a humming of sorts, pricks at my ears. Static. Until she suddenly shouts at me. *Why aren't you listening to me, Lenore? You never listen.*

It was the same in Dr. Melvin's office. The buzzing static prickling at my ears. His voice barely audible behind it. He too was entombed in a way—like my mother. Hiding behind his credentials. Crouched behind a too large desk in a too brown, too quiet room. We're all keeping secrets, I suppose.

Dr. Melvin was concerned that I hadn't brought anyone with me...to get the news. He brought in a counselor—his secretary, I think. She sat beside me, resting her hand on my arm, ready to console me. I doubt either one of them expected my reaction. Hell, I didn't expect it. It was an exhalation of a sort. A relief. Death points to such ultimate finality, doesn't it? And even though I couldn't hear him saying the words, they were all around me just the same. Cancer.

Advanced. Little to be done. I thanked him and left the building, found my car and sat in it, the windows up. Cars in Florida, in the summer months, become ovens—death traps for dogs and babies unfortunate enough to be at the mercy of vile creatures.

But the heat has its attributes. Suffocation is, I mean to say, not only death. Heat can cleanse the soul as it burns the skin. I liked to breathe it in for as long as I could stand it. That day, I could only manage a few seconds before I felt like I was choking. I started the engine, put the air conditioning on full blast and drove home—it would begin to cool the car just as I entered my neighborhood near the bay. Sycamore Street might have had a few sycamores in its heyday—back when it was new and clever. Now my house was like all the others: crusty, peeling, losing itself with age. I was glad to be home, though.

The world looked different as I climbed out of the car and locked it up. Bright. Brighter than I remembered. I realized, as if I'd never known, that I had very little grass in the yard. Not even many weeds. Somehow the sand in my flip flops never bothered me before when I walked around to the back of the house. But that day I wanted to buy a flatbed loaded with sod on pallets and watch strong, sweaty men lay it down. I wanted to stand outside every morning and evening and watch sprinklers bring green life to my yard. But it was too late for all of that.

I squeezed my way through the back entrance to the house, wended the path amid the walls and mounds of my shelter and found my spot in the front room on the sofa in front of the television—out of breath. It would be over soon, I thought, and it was comforting. I turned to look at the stacks of boxes, books, and whatnot—piled to the ceiling, my mountain of filth—and considered toppling it. It would be a fitting end. But I knew I didn't deserve a fitting end. And we all should get what we deserve. I really wanted to do only one thing before I left the earth—and I'd done a powerful job of ensuring I'd never be able to do it. So I sat like a lump, surrounded by my fears, and waited.

Sometime later, perhaps a week, my neighbor Mel showed up at the back door with her daughter, Hannah. It was only then I realized school had ended for the summer and I wondered at what point I'd stopped measuring my days and years by the public school calendar.

Mel was smiling, as usual, without a hint of duplicity, which made it all the more suspect. But the girl, Hannah, was as sour as any teenager on television. Her hair bleached blond with a dark part across the top of her head. Gloating with the superiority all kids her age manage to wield. Hannah hated her mother—that much had been obvious from the start. But she hated me more. I always felt good about that. Mel could find some consolation in it, I hoped. I let them in. Turned my back on them to lead them through the cave into the front room where they had to stand in what little space I'd been comfortable not filling. The look on the girl's face—priceless. I'd say it was terror of a sort. Mel, the natural chocolate brunette that Hannah no doubt was, underneath, was able to keep her bluff; but then, she'd been inside my house before.

I'll do my best to explain. I'm what you'd call a hoarder. I'm not one of those you see on television who deny it. I don't like to say I'm a collector. I get it. I'm a hoarder—a hamster in a cage. And in one corner of it, my house, I've built my nest. I don't pretend to care for the things I used to build it—newspapers (my mother's choice, but arriving thinner and thinner these days, not the fat folded behemoths they once were), clothing (mostly used and smelling of old people; I get it at thrift stores), broken, cheap trinkets (figurines, movie memorabilia, salt and pepper shakers, those cheap snow globes you can get at the dollar store— isn't it odd that the dollar store sells the same stuff that used to litter the dime stores of our youths?), office supplies, books, magazines. Lord knows what all's in there. I built it in the back of my mind, not the front. It's done instinctively, like the birds with twigs, piece by piece. I hate it all because I know what it ought to do to me, if it were conscious. I want to scream at it, tell it to leave me alone. But if you tried to take any part of it, I'd fight you, because, I think...this mountain of stuff is my art—it's the insides of me, the guts, the real trash that makes me, me.

"I was worried," Mel said. And she looked it.

"You think I was dead? The house stink of death from the outside, does it?" I laughed, startling Hannah and that made me laugh more.

Mel was pink in the face. That's the thing about Florida. You can't walk outside your house in the summer months without breaking out in a sweat. Walk across your yard to pay a neighborly visit and you run the risk of sun stroke. "No, no, not at all." She winced. "Your newspapers are piling up on the driveway. Is everything all right?"

"You bring the girl to help you carry out the body?" You should know that I am fully aware of the way I speak to people—as if I'm ignorant. I do it on purpose. I don't know why. It started after I retired and began working more feverishly at the cocoon.

A tinkly sort of nervous laugh came out of Mel. "Don't be silly, Mrs. Hawn. I came to see if you're all right."

"Well, I'm not. I've got the cancer. I'm dying."

Silence hung around for several seconds too long. Silence in a hoard is different from any silence in the world. Outside, you must know, silence is nonexistent. There are always cars. If you get away enough, wind whispers, birds call, and creatures shake the bushes. Inside, your refrigerator hums and knocks. The kick and rush of your air conditioner when it comes on passes you by as if it never happened. The television drones, maybe. Voices behind doors echo. Tiny ticks of clocks. In a hoard, though—in a densely packed maze of paper, cloth, plastic, and ceramic—deafening silence startles your senses. The sort of nothing that stops your heart before disaster strikes. And there we were, the three of us, standing in it.

I watched the girl. She was the sort you knew just by looking at her. It was all blatant, all over her face, and in her hands the way they rubbed at her elbows as she wrapped her arms around herself. She wanted everyone to know how strong she was, how independent, how little she needed anyone or anything. She wanted us all to leave her the fuck alone (I'm cheating here, of course—I've heard the girl scream that dozens of times at her mother). But it was plain she didn't mean any of it.

"Is there anything I can do to help?" Mel said, finally.

"I'm tired." I shuffled through some of the debris on the floor to my spot on the sofa and fell into it. Picked up the remote and clicked the television back on. "Wasting away, anymore. I could use somebody to help me with the cats." At that, Hannah's head turned this way and that. She liked cats, I could see. "I can't get down to do the scooping," I said. "Leastwise, I can't get back up too easy once I'm down."

"Hannah would be happy to help," Mel said.

I laughed. Loud. Mothers love to volunteer other people for stuff like that, don't they? In a way, I was disappointed in Mel for doing it. But then I got the idea she had a motive. It was almost as if it were true what some people say...that everything happens for a reason, that the universe is working everything out and we're just pawns in its game.

Those first few days, the girl showed up but didn't talk. Her mouth and nose pinched up a little at the odor, and her eyes watered from the dust. I knew, over time, she'd get used to it. It's not a dumpster feel, exactly. It's a lived in, cat house, flea market sort of atmosphere. It grows on you. And sure, I lived with bugs. Lots of roach carcasses littering window sills and pooled in corners. Some flies. Gnats.

I showed her where I kept the bag of food—on the table in the kitchen, atop boxes and stacks of magazines and mail. I had a roll of masking tape, somewhere, I told her; she'd need it to patch up any holes the cats might have chewed in the bag.

"They're fat," I told her. "And they knock all this stuff off when they jump up to get at it. You'll have to pick it all up for me."

She nodded and poured kibble into the two bowls on the floor in front of the sink. She washed out the big plastic water bowl, refilled it, and put it down in front of the stove. Then she stood there, waiting to see if the cats would come out of hiding. I'm sure she suspected it was a hoax—the cats didn't exist, except perhaps in my head. But she scooped the boxes sure enough. I wondered if she considered the lengths a dying old woman might go to—what might she be scooping out of the sand if not cat piss and shit? What if I was as crazy as my house?

On the fourth day, for whatever reason, the cats showed up out of the hoard and sniffed at her. The girl's face nearly tore apart. They don't care much for smiling when adults are around, these teenagers. She squatted in the tiny space available in my kitchen and let them rub against her.

"Fat one's Schrodinger," I told her. "And the other fat one is Darwin."

Schrodinger was a black and white tuxedo with white whiskers. Darwin was a rich chocolate brown. When they went to eating, Hannah stood and turned to me.

The first thing she said to me, ever, was, "I expected this place to smell worse."

I can't blame her for that. But one day, about a week into her assignment, she stood in the tiny space of my front room, wiping her washed hands on a paper towel, looking around at the walls of trash, then looked at me and said, "What happened to you?"

2.

They don't ever ask that, you know. "What happened to you?" They might ask, "What happened *here*?" which is an accusation really, something you say to a five-year-old when you discover him in the hallway with a crayon in his hand. But more often, they try to ignore it. They assume you're insane, mentally disturbed, or just overly untidy. Nobody ever asks, "What happened to you?" So, I was unprepared. I said, "What happened to *you*?" right back. This was something she could understand, I suppose, as it was childish.

She rolled her eyes. "I'm being punished. Wouldn't be here otherwise. Mel thinks this'll teach me good."

"For climbing out your window in the middle of the night?"

Her eyes popped open, mouth too, like she'd discovered I had brains in my head where she thought there must be wool.

"That's right," I teased her. "I seen you plenty." As it happened, my bathroom window looked across our side lawns to her bedroom. Granted, I had to climb onto the pile of clothes in the tub to see out of it. She and that nose-ringed boy couldn't be quiet if you gagged them. "So, your mother's making you do the community service, is that it?"

She nodded.

"Well, you could have it worse, you know."

She gave off a little harrumph.

"You could be pregnant," I said. "On the streets. Strung out on drugs. What is the drug of choice for you kids these days? Cocaine?"

She chuckled. "I don't think so."

"Crack?"

"I don't know."

"They don't let me buy Sudafed anymore at the store. I have to ask the pharmacist and show my ID and then I can only buy so much before they think I'm cooking it into something. What is it they're making out of it?"

"I told you I don't know. I don't do drugs."

"Bullshit."

She stared at me; she knew I'd seen her. They all knew. What? Did they think I was an idiot? Okay, the kids think I'm nuts. I can't blame them. There's a park across the street, thirty yards north of my house. It used to be an empty lot until its numbskull owner gifted it to the city. So what do they do with it? Put a park in the middle of a lower class neighborhood. It's good for the kids, they said. Sure, sure. But not so good for people trying to get some peace and quiet during the daytime. I've come out of my house a few times screaming at them to shut the hell up. I might have done it in a nightgown, with a shower cap on my head, once or twice. Might have had a broom in my hand. It's the little things in life that make it interesting. They toss eggs at my house on Halloween and then some of the parents force some of the kids over the next day to clean it all up. I scream at the parents, too. You get to be something of a legend if you work at it. Anyway, I'd stormed over there plenty of times when the older kids were out after dark, smoking weed.

14

"Pot doesn't count," she said. She blushed. Because, of course it did.

"They say it's a gateway drug. You know what that means?"

"No." She was scowling, like they do.

"It means before you know it, you'll be passed out in an alleyway with needle holes in your arm."

"That's just stupid."

"Of course it is," I nearly shouted at her. "There ain't no alleyways in Strawbridge."

I glared at her, eyebrows pulled tight, lips pursed, but she was slow on the take. So, I raised my brows and smiled.

Finally, another crack in her ceramic façade. She giggled. "Well, it ought to be legal anyway, right?"

"But you'd still be too young to smoke it, even if it was. What are you? Sixteen?"

"Seventeen."

"You drive?"

Her face fell and she shook her head. "Mel won't let me get my license."

"The pot thing, right?"

"She doesn't know about that. You aren't going to tell her, are you?"

"Do I look like the sociable type?"

She looked me over, thinking about it. I spent my days in what they call house dresses. They buttoned up the front, or zipped—I confess I rather like a thirty-six-inch zipper. The dresses hung down to my knees or below. The fabric on the backside of each one was wearing out, I admit. But I was fifty-five. I could sit around all day if I wanted. And anyway, I was dying. Who cared if I did my hair or put on powder? Or brushed my teeth? Granted, I hadn't done any of those things regularly for quite some time and it occurred to me, just then, with Hannah giving me that my-God-you're-a-mess sneer, that the cancer had finally given my entire lifestyle an excuse.

"I won't tell her," I said.

"Are you all right?"

"What?"

"You look like...sad."

I shrugged and looked around. Next to the girl, Schrodinger was curled up on a trash bag full of something soft, probably that fabric I bought on sale, thinking I'd clean out one of the bedrooms and make myself something. When was that? When was it that I felt like I had a life? "I'm fine. Just tired."

She reached down and scratched at Schrodinger's neck. "All right. I'll see you tomorrow morning." She was tired of talking to the crazy old woman. Who could blame her? As she turned to leave, I stopped her.

"I'll pay you," I said.

"I can't take money. This is supposed to be a lesson or something." More rolling of the eyes.

"No. I'll pay you to do something for me." I had her attention now. Pot isn't cheap, is it? "I need you to find something for me."

"What?"

"A box. A wood box. The kind you get up in the mountains. I got it at Chimney Rock when I was a kid."

"Wait a minute," she said. "You want me to find something...in here?" She grimaced and looked around the cocoon.

I nodded.

"Do you know where it is?"

"I think so. Should be in the master bedroom."

She backed up a bit and peered down the hallway—a tiny tunnel, barely a person wide—and shook her head. "Can I even get into it?"

"That's why I'll pay you. It'll take some work."

"How much?"

"A hundred dollars."

Her eyes flew wide. "Seriously?"

"Yep."

"Must be really important."

"It is."

"You gonna tell me why?"

"I don't see where that's any of your business."

Her face twisted up a bit, brows tortured, lips sucked in. "All right."

"But you can't throw anything out."

"I've seen the show," she said. "I know how it works."

3.

I want to start with Oliver, even though he is not the beginning. Oliver is...or should have been, the end, and so I think it's proper to start with him. I'd known Oliver for several years before he first spoke to me. In Sandy Point, most everybody knew one another, really, so it wasn't that unusual to know a person without really knowing him. The first time he spoke to me was on the bus to the high school, when we were seniors. I'd just moved in with my dad and riding the bus was new. I don't recall seeing Oliver the first two days. But I was still in shock, even though I was cleared to go back to school, so I suppose I wouldn't have noticed. On my third day back at school, he sat beside me—up to then, everybody left me alone on the bench seat—and introduced himself.

"Oliver," he said.

I looked him over and nodded.

"My mother died two years ago," he said.

I blinked slowly, frowning. I tried not to say anything. But he sat there waiting. So, I said, "Did she suffocate under her own hoard of newspapers and cookie sheets?"

"No."

"Then shut up."

The thing about Oliver, though, was that he wouldn't shut up. He was like a fat puppy, bounding around at your heels, happy all the time, trying to get you to laugh and smile and play. And hell, it's a puppy, so what choice do you have?

Oliver was a pale blond with a round face and large straight teeth. He was tall and athletic—on all the sports teams possible in school. I was neither athletic, nor a pretty cheerleader—the important things to be in high school.

This was the late Seventies, so they hadn't invented Goth Chicks yet. But I'd have been one. I might have even cut myself on a more regular basis if I'd known it was a thing to do. My hair, which I'd dyed black the day after my mother died—an action that had its reward in bringing my stepmother, Jennie, to terrified tears—was long and stringy. I wore over-sized tees with holes in them and too-long corduroys shredded at the cuffed hems. I didn't want to be seen. I was perturbed that Oliver saw me—that he had the nerve to speak to me. So I ignored him and he would have none of it. He passed me in the hallways, between all my classes, it seemed, and said hello, smiling. He found me at lunch, hidden on the west side of the band and chorus building, and sat with me, watching me nibble at a cafeteria peanut butter cookie. It would take him a week to ask me why I never ate a proper lunch.

"What's proper?" I said.

"Sandwich."

"Sandwich," I said with a laugh and rolled my eyes.

"Did you know," he said, slapping bread crumbs from his hands, "that we're the only two students at Sandy Point whose mothers have died?"

I glared at him.

"My mom had ovarian cancer." That he could say that without emotion told me a lot of things that I was too young to comprehend.

We stared at each other for several seconds and I

watched as his face betrayed him. Just for a second, before he managed another smile.

I think I started breathing then. I mean, really breathing. For the first time in a long time. Maybe it was a combination, you know? Of my mother dying, of moving into my father's house with its sparse decor, into a bedroom with nothing but a bed and a desk and a bookcase, nothing littering the floor, no boxes and piles of clothing to climb over—the sort of situation that at first made me tremble and want to drop my head into the toilet bowl—and Oliver sitting there in front of me in pain—a pain he didn't want to share. I breathed because I realized I felt no pain. I had no right to suffocate. I had to breathe like everybody else. Does that make sense? I don't know.

"I could drive you to school," he said.

That was Oliver. He was always out of the blue, as if things popped into his head at odd moments and he had no compulsion to keep them where they belonged.

"I thought," he said, "maybe you'd rather not ride the bus."

"You have a car?"

He nodded.

"Why are you riding the bus, then?"

He looked at me, a sheepish grin unfolding onto the bottom of his face.

"You're telling me," I said, "you started riding the bus because my mom died?"

He shrugged. "It's stupid, isn't it? But nobody else really gets it."

"What makes you think *you* get it?"

"I've been there."

I shook my head. "It's not the same." I grabbed my baggy, blue denim purse and stood up, wadding the wax paper my cookie had come enveloped in, into a ball. "Your mom died a normal death. She was probably beautiful and brave and she fought to live for you. My mom wore the same ratty cotton dress for fifty-nine weeks straight, stank of booze, and died under her filthy hoard of newspapers. Newspapers that she cared about more than anything in the world, including me."

He stood too, frowning. "But either way, we both lost our moms."

"My mom was a freak. I'm better off without her."

"You don't mean that." He stepped closer and reached out to touch my arm.

"You don't get anything, Oliver."

We walked in silence, on our way to class, until we parted. Went our separate ways. I wanted it to stay that way, but Oliver had different ideas. The next morning, I stood at the bus stop yawning, ignoring the other students gathered there. They acted as if I had a disease and I thought maybe I did. Maybe that was what Oliver was talking about. The thing we shared—the way people looked at you after death has tainted you. But it was impossible. Oliver was popular; he had friends. He was one of them. The sports kids, the cheerleader kids, the well-dressed, good-looking kids. But maybe he felt diseased.

It was at about that point, when I was thinking about the disease of death, that Oliver pulled up to the curb in a little blue car. He honked, leaned over to the passenger side and pushed open the door.

"Come on," he said.

Everybody turned to glare at me. I didn't know why I got in. I've had a lot of years to think about it. A lot of time to work out my motivations. Was I weak? Did I want to be part of that crowd? Did I like him? Want to date him? I don't think so. I think I got into Oliver's car that morning because he was the only person in the world who left openings—long openings heavy with anticipation. He was the only person I knew who seemed to want me to talk.

And as much as I might have convinced myself that I didn't want to talk, something in me disagreed. I needed to empty myself out. And I needed someone to hear it.

4.

Hannah started at the doorway to the master bedroom at the end of the hall. She carried out handfuls of stuff—old mail, bags of clothing, stuffed animals, dolls, cat toys still in the plastic packaging. I stayed in my little hollowed out spot on the sofa, pretending to watch the television. At first she was putting the stuff in the living room, with me, shoving it into bulbous mounds of other stuff. She tossed a bag onto a tall pile—took her a few tries to get it to stay. She put a ceramic cookie jar, shaped like a dog with its paw in the air and missing its lid, on top of the magazines that sat atop the television. But after a few trips, she stood in the little space cradling a bunch of padded envelopes, some stuck closed, hiding treasures, some ripped open, some brand new. A cloud of dust was stirred up now and surrounded her like an aura.

"There isn't going to be room anywhere to put this stuff," she said.

I looked around my sanctuary. It must be part of the mental processes of a hoarder—I thought there was *always* room. Always little corners in which to insert something new.

"Don't bother looking," she said. "I can put this junk

down somewhere, sure. But have you been back there? I can't even see into the room, yet. All of that stuff is not going to fit anywhere else in the house."

I worked hard at finding a solution. The garage was out, of course. It was the first space I'd crammed full. The attic, too, was stuffed—you could see cracks in the ceiling where it threatened to vomit my things out. The sheds out back were filled. The yard was out. I'd been fined too many times. I could say it was temporary, but I knew the neighbors would call the county as soon as they started seeing piles of stuff appear.

"You're going to have to let me throw some of it away," she said.

"No."

"Then I can't find the box." She appeared to be upset about it. Not typical teenage behavior at all, if you ask me. But money will do strange things even to teenagers.

"I'm not paying you if you don't," I told her.

"Well then—" she dropped the padded envelopes to the floor at her feet— "you'll never find the box."

A threat? I sat there fuming. It was as if the girl knew I had to have it—knew I was desperate.

She climbed over some of my piles and perched herself on the far edge of the sofa. "I know you're attached to this stuff."

"I'm not attached."

"Then why can't I throw it away?"

"It's not the stuff."

"Then what?" She was exasperated. I guess I couldn't blame her. Even I knew it didn't make sense.

"I can't explain it. I just need the stuff in here."

"But it's in the back room. You never go in there, right? You wouldn't even know I'm emptying it out."

"I'll feel it."

"Oh, my God." She stood and tried to stomp over all

my trash and boxes, but fell and slid forward toward the kitchen. "This is stupid." She got herself on all fours and managed to stand, teetering a bit on the avalanche she'd created. "What do you care, anyway? You're dying. What do you need with all this crap now?"

I stared at her for a moment, trying to think of some way out of it. She was right, of course. If you're willing to look at death realistically. I'd be in the ground soon enough and all this stuff—this warm, loving, protective, claustrophobic stuff—would be someone else's problem. But I had it in my mind that I would die with it all. The thought of that back room empty, well, it made my breath stagger. I couldn't do it.

"If you hurried," I said. "You could pile it all up in the back yard, find the box, and get it all back inside the room before the neighbors find out and report me."

She sucked in a deep breath. She seemed older then. Not so young and rebellious. She was wearing mascara, and it was rubbed off onto the edges of her eyelids and I didn't know if that was on purpose or not. It made her look ...hounded—as if she were keeping something in and someone was hunting her down, prepared to rip it out of her heart. She looked as if she had actually lived a life, at such a young age—and not a good one.

"I could do it," she said, but glared at me. "But not for a hundred."

"Five hundred."

She nodded. "I'll have to tell Mel, though."

"You call your mother Mel? That's a bit disrespectful, ain't it?"

She rolled her eyes. "You want me to do this or not?"

"I said I'd pay you."

"And I'll do what you want; but you don't get to pry into my personal life. You got that? This is a business deal. That's all."

"Fine, then."

"And it's the money." She grabbed a handful of envelopes from the floor and carried them toward the kitchen, disappearing behind stacks of boxes and bags of whatnot. "You tell Mel," she called through the trash, "I'm doing this because you asked me, plain and simple. She doesn't need to know about the money." I heard the back door creak open, whine its way back to the jamb on its spring, and close again.

She went back and forth like that for the rest of the afternoon, until at one point, I heard a crack of thunder and she rushed back into my little spot, wide-eyed.

"It's going to rain all over the stuff."

"A little water never hurt nobody," I said.

"But your stuff. Don't you care?"

Everything tensed up inside me. I wanted to scream, to hit. I wished I had something to bite. "I told you I don't give a damn about the stuff."

She stepped back. Put her hands up, as a defense. "Okay. I'm sorry. But, how am I going to get a soggy mess of trash back inside?"

"Well, that's *your* problem. Ain't it?"

She worked hard and fast for several hours that day and when she left, I went to the back door and peered out into the yard to see what she'd done. Rain pattered at the dirt and tinkled on the roofs of the sheds. Up against the house, Hannah had stacked rows and rows of my possessions. I stepped out onto the little concrete slab and let the screen door click shut behind me. I stood there, fighting with myself—telling myself it would all be back inside soon enough. What difference would a little rain make? But it was no use. I don't think I was aware of what I was doing until I'd carried several armfuls of dolls and magazines back inside. I was hiding it all. And when I found myself on my hands and knees in the kitchen, trying to force open the cabinet under the sink against a pile of canvas shopping bags, and a plastic container of rocks I'd collected out of a stream on a trip up north, I stopped, peered into the crack in the door where several vegetable brushes were trying to escape, and laughed.

5.

I rode to school with Oliver. I let him talk. He told me stories about his cousins up north on a farm. He talked about movies and music. He said his brother played guitar. He told me that he had two dogs, a cat, and a hamster, but the hamster was really his brother's. And he told me that his father was dating a woman who was in college. And after every amusing thing, he'd turn to me with a smile and say, "Can you believe that?" Or, "Can you imagine that?" Then he'd wait and wait for a response, his eyes darting between me and the road. It was annoying.

After a week or so of this, I was sitting in my biology class, last row, far corner. Arianna Carter sat in front of me in that class and I spent a lot of time staring at her hair. It was unreal hair. Straight. Thick. All shades of brown and gold. And three minutes before bell, every day, she'd start running a comb through it...absentmindedly, like it was habit. This particular morning, she was putting on lipstick. She had a compact mirror in her left hand and outlined her lips with a pencil in deep maroon. She pressed them together and popped them open. Then she switched to a lighter brick red in a tube and covered her bottom lip, then the top, opening her mouth wide and getting right up close to the crease between her lips. She caught me in the mirror, staring, and turned in her seat.

"You're Lenore," she said.

I'd been sitting behind her since August. I was in her English and American Government classes last year, and had gym with her freshman year. I nodded. Yes, I'm Lenore.

"Are you dating Oliver?"

My mouth fell open and I felt my cheeks redden as I struggled to find an answer to that.

"You're riding to school with him." It was an accusation. She sat there, her eyebrows lifted, lips pursed, like she'd scolded me and was waiting for my excuses.

"We're just friends."

She nodded, slowly. "I figured."

When I told Oliver about it on the way home, he laughed.

"What's funny?"

"She figured," he mused. "What's that supposed to mean?"

"It means I'm a loser and of course you wouldn't date me."

"You're not a loser."

I stared at the road as he drove, watching it disappear under the car. I liked to keep my eyes on the road, even tried not to blink. Something was wrong with Sandy Point. The buildings were sad, droopy; they begged me to help them and I didn't know what I could do about it. Even though the sun was shining, the town oozed a dreariness that I related to...and I didn't want to relate. I didn't want Sandy Point to commiserate. I wanted to be left alone in my perpetual sour mood. I didn't know why that was so hard for the town to understand. Of course, I knew, even then, that this sort of thinking was crazy. It was only a matter of time, I assumed, before someone found out and I'd be put out of my misery.

Oliver liked Sandy Point. You could tell. The way he was always looking around, smiling, pointing out failed businesses, or new sidewalks. That day, as usual, he was easy and relaxed, tapping his thumbs on the steering wheel to the music on the radio. At one point he reached over, turned it up loud, and sang the chorus, before lowering the volume again. He was the most annoying person I'd ever met. I started shaking my head back and forth faster and faster; I closed my eyes and sighed.

"What is it?" he said.

"I just don't understand what this is all about." My voice was much harsher than I'd intended. I calmed myself down. "I don't even know why I ride to school with you."

He didn't respond right away, which was unusual, and when I looked at him, his jaw was set. I was worried he was angry and not sure why it should bother me.

"Maybe I'm good company," he said.

"I guess."

"Maybe I'm cute." He was smirking.

I rolled my eyes.

"Maybe you like me."

"I do not," I blurted out. "I mean, I do. Of course I do. But not like...not like that."

"I don't see why not." He was still smiling. "Other girls like me."

"Arianna Carter being one."

We were quiet for a bit, until he turned onto our street. "Well," he said and paused. Then he pulled up to the curb at my dad's house and turned to me. "I like *you*."

"Sure you do," I said with a laugh. "Because I'm so likable."

"You don't think you're good enough for me."

"I didn't say that." But it was true enough. I pulled at the door handle.

"Let's get together Saturday."

"What for?"

"Come on. There's a party at Fox Lake."

I stepped out of the car and leaned back in. "I don't like parties. But thanks, anyway." I tried not to slam the car door, but I did.

As I walked to the front door, hearing his car purring in the street the whole time, I realized I was flush and trembling. Did Oliver Stanton just ask me out? It had to be some kind of sick joke. Like that movie Carrie, except that I couldn't move things with my mind and I'd been menstruating by that time for five years. It didn't make sense. I couldn't wrap my head around it. I needed time to mull it over, to brood, and find some dark music to remind me of who I really was. Unfortunately, when I walked into the house, Jennie was waiting for me. She peeked behind me at Oliver's car, still sitting at the curb.

"That's the Stanton boy, isn't it?" she said.

I nodded. Who talked like that? The Stanton boy? This was the Seventies, not the Fifties.

"Your dad says you've been riding to school with him."

I walked down the hallway to my room; she followed. I tossed my purse onto my bed and put my books on the desk.

"You want to talk about it?" she said.

"About what?" I stood at the foot of my bed, scowling.

"Okay," she said. "Listen, you can...you know...decorate your room. If you want. You don't have to leave it...bare."

I nodded. When she left, I closed and locked the bedroom door and dropped to the floor. I sat there for about an hour until I heard the bus from the elementary school stop at the corner. David and Paige came bounding down the hall yelling about spiders at the school. Or bees. Something stupid. I sat with my back against my bedroom door until my dad came home from work and Jennie called me for dinner. I got up, shook off the numbness and walked out into the dining room where they all stopped what they were doing—setting the table, carrying dishes of food out from the kitchen—and stared at me.

"I'm going out," I said.

I left the house and walked to Oliver's, four doors down, across the street. He was surprised to see me on his front porch, but he didn't seem to mind it.

"You change your mind about Saturday?"

"I did."

"Come on in."

They were all gathered in the family room, on the sofa and in recliners, tray tables in front of them, eating tacos and watching television. His dad, plump and balding. His brother, older, but pretty much a replica of Oliver. His grandmother who'd been a teacher of mine in elementary school. The room was cluttered. Needed dusting. A stack of books stood, edges jutting this way and that, on the floor in front of an overfilled book case. Again, I felt myself breathe. That was when I knew for certain that I was going to tell Oliver.

6.

The girl didn't notice that I'd taken some of the stuff back inside; at least, she didn't say anything if she did. But there was something more important to notice. Overnight, the wind whipped up and spread some of my papers and bits of trash across the yard. Hannah stomped in the next morning saying she was going to have to put the loose stuff in trash bags. She spent the rest of that day doing that, slapping open white plastic bags and stuffing them full, tying them off with the yellow plastic ribbon handles, until the rain came again. And after she went home, I puttered around, pulling at the knots she'd made—tight, impenetrable—reaching in where I could make an inconspicuous hole and pulling out a spool of thread or a figurine of a dancing lady, before giving up and just standing on the porch slab looking at the bags, listening to the song the rain made on the plastic, and on the dirt, on the sheds.

The next day, Hannah arrived in a light mood, as if the rain had cleaned something away. She fed the cats and scooped their boxes, with them both underfoot. Schrodinger and Darwin liked the company, the newness of another smell, different fingernails scratching behind their ears. But they could only take so much before they were off again, finding their hiding places in the hoard. Hannah then searched the house for more trash bags.

"How do you find anything in this mess?"

"I know where everything is," I told her. I was pretending to watch *The Price is Right.*

She'd perched on the edge of the sofa again, her backside up against a pile of books.

"So, where are the trash bags?"

I tried to make a grumbling sound, the kind of noise I imagined really old people make to teenagers who pester them. "You'll have to get some more."

"I'll tell Mel to do it. It won't be until Saturday."

"What the hell blazes?" I'd been practicing that ever since the day I saw her climbing out her window at two in the morning with that creepy young man she hung out with. "What the hell blazes?" I'd whispered. I liked it and said it sometimes to the cats, the television, a pile of something that toppled and fell.

She smiled. "What do you want me to do? I'm not walking. It's all the way to the other side of town."

"Don't you have a car?"

"You know I don't."

"Get that boyfriend of yours to take you."

She rolled her eyes at me. "He's out of town."

"He's in prison, ain't he?"

"He is not. I'm not allowed to ride in his car anymore, anyway. It's just going to have to wait."

"God damn it," I said and lifted myself off the couch with a groan. "I'll take you. But I'll have to put something decent on."

I eased myself around the table in front of the sofa, bumping a stack of magazines, spilling several onto the floor. I reached for the pile of clothing on top of four large boxes on the other side of the television, in the corner.

"Some of your walls," she said, "are made completely

out of junk."

"I like it that way. This house, it was what you'd call an open plan. You'd walk in the front door—over behind those boxes—and you could see the kitchen, the back door, this room here, and even a bit down the hallway there."

"I can't even *see* the front door."

"It's there." I chuckled. "But this way—" I pulled a pair of cotton twill pants from the clothes pile—"is better. This way, I got this little room. All walled off nice and quiet. Now you go on. I'll meet you out front by the car."

She stood. "Couldn't the walls...fall?"

I stared at her, not able to answer.

"I mean," she said. "Isn't it dangerous?"

I looked around the tiny space and felt small. Whenever I remembered my mother, suffocating under the avalanche of her own hoard, I felt tiny amid my own. "I think that might be the whole point of it."

She smirked at me and made her way out through the towers of stuff, shaking her head.

When I'd changed, found my bag and wallet, and met her at the car, my old blue four-door, she was standing in the driveway, smoking a cigarette—her free arm wrapped around her waist, her other elbow propped on it, the cigarette nestled between her fingers.

"I suppose you think you look grown up doing that?"

She exhaled a puff of smoke and flicked some ash, watching it blow across the driveway in the wind.

"You been crying or something?" I asked her.

She stubbed the cigarette out with her shoe and started for the passenger side.

"Hold on," I said. "You pick that up."

She sighed and did as she was told. "What do you want me to do with it?"

"That ain't my problem. Put it in your pocket. Put it in your mouth. I don't care."

She stood, glaring, watching me as I got out my keys and unlocked the doors. "Oh for Christ's sake," I said. "There's a trash bag in the car."

I eased my way into the front seat and started tossing stuff off her seat, throwing it into the back.

"You filled up your car, too?"

I mimicked, "You filled up your car, too?"

"That's real mature," she said as she slid into the passenger side.

I reached behind her seat and pulled out an old McDonald's bag. "Here."

She deposited her butt and I stuffed the bag back behind her seat. I slammed my door shut and waited for her to do the same, but she just sat there.

"Well?" I said.

"I'm waiting for you to start the engine," she said. "Turn the AC on."

"Nope. Close the door."

You'd have thought I was crazy, the look she gave me; but she closed the door. Sweat beaded up on my temples and I breathed in the hot air. She started to roll down her window and, without thinking, I reached over and grabbed at her arm.

"Put it back up," I said.

"Are you crazy? It's hot as hell in here."

I squeezed—threatened her arm with my fingernails.

"For God's sake." She rolled it up. "I can't breathe."

I closed my eyes.

"Mrs. Hawn."

I sighed. It wasn't the same with a pissy little girl in the car anyway, so I started up the engine and turned the air on.

"Thank God," she said. "How old is this thing, any-way?"

"No point in buying a new car now, is there?"

That shut her up. As I drove us to the store, her silence

pricked at me. The trouble with people, mostly, is that they're always talking—always yakking about something or other. It's that they don't know what else to do, I think. But Hannah sat very still in the car, her eyes on the road ahead. I struggled to come up with some topic of conversation, but I was unpracticed.

Finally, she said, "This is weird."

"What's weird?"

"I don't know. Me, here, in your car."

"What's weird about that?"

"Nothing."

"No, you started it. What's weird?"

She fumed for a moment or two.

"Tell me," I said.

"I don't even know you." She looked at me. "I mean. You've been our neighbor since I can even remember. But nobody knows you. Everybody's scared of you; did you know that?"

"Are you scared? Is that it?"

"I'm not scared."

Then we were quiet again. When we finally turned into the Walmart lot, I parked, shut off the engine and sat still. She did, too, which I found somehow comforting—as if maybe she understood the heat like I did.

"I know they're scared," I said. "I guess I wanted them scared." I turned to her. She was smiling at me. Her lips parted; she laughed.

"One Halloween," she said. "Just before dark, you came outside in a clown mask."

"I remember. You were, what...ten?"

"You scared the crap out of this little snot; what was his name? God, we all hated him."

I nodded. "He was the brat who pulled his pants down and peed in my front yard every day for a month."

"Until that Halloween."

I took the keys from the ignition and pushed the door open.

As we walked toward the store, Hannah said, "He's in jail."

There was something strangely sweet about her confessing to me. "What'd he do?"

"Broke into some houses."

"You with him?"

She was quiet.

"I won't tell on you. But you think about where you want to be in twenty years. You stick with that little shit, it won't be anywhere pretty."

"Like I have a lot of choices," she said.

I stopped, right there in the middle of the parking lot, a car waiting for us to move. "You got choices."

"Come on." She put her hand on my arm and pulled me forward. "You don't have to be, like, my mom or anything. Why do grownups think they have to parent everybody's kid?"

I thought about it, as we made our way through the store, arguing about where we'd find the big trash bags. Once we were back at my house, and I felt that compulsive urge to get back inside fast, to curl up in my spot, surrounded by my safety, my protection, I realized the truth of it.

"I'm sorry," I told her as we made our way around to the back door.

"About what?"

"I'm one to talk about choices. About making a life."

She chuckled. "Maybe you are the one. You're the 'don't let this happen to you' poster."

"It don't work like that."

"Why not?"

"My mother was a hoarder. As bad as me. And I followed. I did what she did. It don't work."

"Not for your kids maybe. Do you have kids?"

I shook my head. We stood at the back door, both of us looking at the piles of stuff Hannah had already taken from the back room.

"But it works for other people," she said.

"Why's that?" I unlocked the door and pushed it open as far as it would go—just enough for us to slide through.

"I don't know." She went ahead of me into the cave, turning sideways to maneuver through the stacks and piles. "I think it's because we get...what's the word? Imprinted. That's it. We get imprinted, like those ducklings in that science experiment."

"I got no idea what you're talking about," I lied.

"We take on the behaviors of our parents, whether we like it or not. If your parents smoke, you'll probably smoke. It's...habit or something. But other people—" She stopped at the entrance to my hovel and opened the box of trash bags— "we see them and think, 'I don't want to turn out like that.' And we learn from it."

"But your mother didn't get mixed up with the likes that boyfriend of yours, did she? She's been on her own for as long as I've known her and that's hard. Looks to me like she's done a good job with you. Your mother is a good woman."

Her face went slack. "I'll get back to it."

She took a few bags down into the hall and left me standing there wondering what I'd missed.

7.

It was that Saturday, when Oliver took me out to Fox Lake—I stood next to him, slightly behind, as he talked with his friends, feeling out of place—that I started telling. I knew I couldn't get right to the heart of it; I wasn't sure I would be able to tell that part at all. I had to build up to it. And it was as if Oliver knew. As if he knew exactly what the trouble was and how to get at it. After we'd each had a beer, we left the party and walked the perimeter of the park. He took my hand and I let him. He talked about school, about college, and then he said, "Tell me about your mom. Why do you think you're better off without her?"

"Does that bother you?"

"A little."

"It's not the kind of thing we're supposed to say out loud."

"It's not the kind of thing we're supposed to believe," he said.

We walked for another minute in silence, until I was ready to tell.

"My mother didn't like me," I said. I inhaled slightly. Waiting. I'd been brave enough to confess such a thing before. Twice. And each time it was met with a scold. Of course your mother liked you. How dare you say such a thing? But Oliver said nothing. He let that space hover, asking for me to fill it.

It would be easy enough to say that my life was perfect before my mother went crazy; but it would be a lie. It looked perfect. We lived in a nice house, in a nice neighborhood in Sandy Point—my father and mother, me and my brother Will. I learned early on that it was Will my mother loved. I was an afterthought. I was only what they needed to make a fourth. Of course, even my father preferred Will. I had no interest in baseball, after all. The truth of it was that I preferred Will as much as my parents did. It was Will, two years older, who told me stories in the dark of our bedrooms on stormy nights. Will walked me to school, defended me from bullies, shared his lunch. Will might have brought us all together, molding us into something like a family, if he'd had the chance.

My mother went crazy on Thursday morning, July 18, 1968. Sure, you might say she had the seeds planted long before. Something must have been lurking inside her, waiting for an impetus—something that cracked and split. But I was seven years old. To my eyes, she went crazy that morning at about ten-thirty, when I watched her scream and run up and down the beach at the shoreline. We'd gone for the morning, to get some sun, have a day away from the house for a change. Dad was working, of course. It was just my mother and me and Will. Will was in the water before we'd found a spot for the blanket. Mom spread it out, letting it fly up into the air and billow down onto the sand. I sat at the edge, careful not to let my feet touch it. It would be covered in sand within minutes, I knew, and she would be angry. She sat, too, and lathered on suntan lotion, watching Will slapping at the water, diving under the surf and rising again like a dolphin. We were normal. And almost anything that might come at us, I figure, we could have weathered. I might have come out all right in the end. Except for that one thing. You don't get over that.

It happened in an instant. One second, I was watching a group of kids playing with a beach ball down the way, and the next, my mother grabbed my arm. My life was over.

"Where's your brother?"

I can still hear the panic in her voice. Still see a stranger, tall, dark-haired, wet, carrying Will's lifeless body in his arms, falling to his knees in the white, hot sands. The screaming. And then silence.

My mother went quiet, inside and out. I hovered on the edges, waiting to be needed, looking for that opening to comfort her that never came. It was my aunt Bridgett who first touched me, pulled me into her arms and cried against the top of my head. But that was three days later; by that time I'd boarded up whatever there was to share.

I went to school when it started, a few weeks later, walked alone, and I saw the way the adults looked at me—I suppose it was compassion in their eyes and on their faces, but it felt like an invasion. An alien seeking a way to burrow itself into my skin. I turned away from it. At home, my mother's smiles never reached her eyes. The obligatory welcome home hugs were never quite complete—no squeeze at the end, no palms, only arms. Will's bedroom door was always closed.

One day, I'd got it into my head that Will was still alive. He was in his room, hiding. It was storming. Lightning flashing outside my bedroom window in the middle of the night. I got up, crossed the hall, and went into his room. In the dark, with only the lightning and the street lamp outside casting shadows, I could see that his room had changed. Things had been shifted. It was as if I'd gone into the wrong room. It frightened me, so I went quickly back to bed. But the next morning, I opened the door again and saw the truth of it.

She'd been out shopping, I guessed, while I was at school. On the bed, she'd laid out clothing—stuff I'd never seen. Blue jeans, t-shirts, button ups. On his desk were stacks of books—Heinlein, Vonnegut, and Le Guin, his favorites. Comic books, too, a stack of them laid edge to spine. A bin in the corner was filled with rolled up posters, too many to fit on his walls. At the foot of his bed was an easel and on the floor, propped up against it sat a dozen white canvases. Once, just before he drowned, I remembered, Will said he wanted to learn to paint.

The hair on the back of my neck tickled and the air in the room shifted.

"Get out," she seethed at the doorway. "Get out and don't come in here again."

I ran past her, to my room, flung myself onto my bed and tried to cry, but I suppose there was too much inside me and too small a space to get out. I felt her heaviness on the bed next to me. She rubbed my back and told me to put on my shoes and meet her at the car. So I did. We went shopping—the first of our regular, almost daily trips. She bought knick-knacks for the living room, utensils and appliances for the kitchen—we had six manual and two electric can openers—sports balls of every sort for Will's room. And she bought me, that first day, three coloring books, a brand new box of sixty-four Crayola crayons with a built-in sharpener, five new dresses, a pair of patent leather shoes, a set of curlers for my hair, and a new bicycle. Not every shopping day was a boon; but every trip we bought at least one new thing.

I felt better—as better as it can feel—while picking something off the shelf. Knowing it was in the car with me as I rode home. Taking it out of the box or bag once there, and setting it in a special place. It was mine. Sometimes I still felt better when I used it. Maybe that first page, the first stroke of wax between the lines or the first few words read.

The first time I rode the bike. But after that, it lagged and the terror returned—it was the terror of knowing Will was gone and not coming back, I think. And so, we went out again.

8.

It was difficult work for the girl. Thin as she was, she had to squeeze her way down the hall to the end where the massive piles of clothing, unopened boxes from Amazon, trinkets tossed into the hoard, and mounds of magazines and newspapers filled the space that was the door to my room of some years ago. Then, I could hear her struggle to pop open the large black trash bag. Bit by bit, I heard the bag being filled. Clothing made soft sounds that reminded me of my father and the muggy hot day he dug up the dirt in the back yard the week after Will drowned. Mother had buried something there—something long, long before. And he dug and dug and never found it. I could tell that my father knew my mother had lost her mind. Trinkets— possibly brass candlesticks—tinkled together inside the bag against the clothing. Paper flitted into the bag like the rustling of doves' wings. And finally that swooshing, ava- lanche of debris and a curse from Hannah.

"Everything all right?" I called, my voice deadened in the cocoon of the living room.

"God damn it!"

I stood and made my way around the coffee table, leaning against the stack of boxes on it for support, and wiggled out of my nest to look down the dark hallway. "You okay?"

She was standing knee deep in paper, struggling to pull the plastic bag out from under the mess. "I'm fine," she said through gritted teeth.

She dug and dug, day after day, hauling out bag after bag of my stuff to the back yard. I went out every day, tugging at the knots she'd tied, making sure they were secure, taping up the holes so rain wouldn't soak the top layers inside. She made progress. And on the third day, she was inside the room itself. She sang, quietly—she didn't think I could hear her, but I did. I hurried to take my seat on the sofa as she entered the hallway. I heard the bag thumping against her legs as she hefted it in front of her, shimmying her way through the tunnel. When she came to the opening in the stacks to the front room, she stopped, dropped the bag, and panting a bit, eased her way around to the sofa and handed me an envelope.

"Looks personal," she said as she went back to retrieve the bag. "It's not even opened yet." When she returned from the back yard, she saw me still holding it. "Well? Aren't you going to read it?"

I shrugged and let it drop to my lap. Every trip the girl made past the living room, on her way into the tunnel and on her way back out with a bag, she looked over at me, her eyes trying to see me over the stack of boxes and bags on the coffee table, to see if I was reading the letter. I wasn't. Then she brought me a card, still in its envelope, unopened. And when she was done for the day, or so she said, hauling out the last bag full of stuff, she brought me a large brown envelope, stiff and hard.

"You ought to at least open this one," she said.

"What for?"

"How can you not open them? Don't you want to know what's inside?"

I shook my head and turned to the television.

"Who are they from?" she said.

I handed her the envelopes. She scanned each one.

"So," she said. "Who's Paige Hawn? She your sister-in-law or something?"

"No."

"Come on, come on," she prodded, excited. "Open them."

I took in a deep breath and let it out. She handed me the small envelope; I turned it over and pulled my finger through the flap, tearing the top open. Pulling out the sheet of notebook paper, trembling, I knew I shouldn't be doing it—I should have thrown them in the trash. I chuckled.

"What?" Hannah said.

"It's all trash, isn't it?" I unfolded the paper and read the letter. Then I handed it to the girl and let her read it.

"Well, she sounds nice. Did you go to her house? Did you have Thanksgiving with them?"

"That letter's from three years ago."

"But, she called, right? After you didn't answer the letter."

"I don't answer the phone. Don't even know for sure where it is."

Hannah looked around the room. Dust from her clearing out down the hall was finding its way into my cubby. She nodded, understanding.

"You should get a cell phone. I could go with you—help you pick one out."

"Who have I got to call?"

"This Paige person, for one. She put her number on it." She showed me the paper, as if I hadn't read it myself already.

"I don't have anything to say to Paige."

"She your sister, then?"

"Half-sister."

"How can you not talk to your sister? If I had a sister, I'd talk to her. I know I would."

"You don't know any such thing."

She sighed. "Maybe you're right."

"Of course I am."

"I guess if she killed somebody..."

"She didn't kill anybody."

"She slept with your boyfriend?"

I rolled my eyes.

"Even then," she said, "that's forgivable by now, right?"

"Nothing to forgive."

She stared at me, like I hadn't given her more than enough information already.

"I'm telling you the truth." I snorted after that, wondering why the hell I had to tell her anything.

"Then call her. What can it hurt?"

"Do I look like a woman in need of company?" I waved my arms around my dim little nest, surrounded by all the comfort I would ever need.

And the girl said, plain as you please, "Yes, actually." She held out the large brown envelope.

"You do it."

She ripped it open like it was Christmas and slid out of it two thin pieces of cardboard. Sandwiched between them was a five-by-seven photograph. Old. Browned with age. My father standing—his dark hair cut close and greased. In his best suit and tie. My mother—her hair piled up and away from the top of her head, a bow stuck at the crease; she's turned slightly, her right hand looped around my father's arm. Me sitting in front of her—so little, so happy, with bangs. And Will. Will, in a suit with a bow tie, hair to match Dad's, nose and eyes like Mom's. Smiling. It was a time captured and frozen, faded, fading. Unreal. I couldn't breathe.

"Who is it?" Hannah asked me.

I shook my head. "Ain't nobody."

9.

Oliver tried to kiss me one morning before school. He'd started coming to the house to pick me up. First he waited in the car. The next day, he got out and stood, leaning against it. The day after that he went up to the door and Jennie let him in. He was part of our morning routine in three days. Of course, I mean their routine. Mine was getting up, waiting for Paige or David to get out of the bathroom, taking a shower, going back into my room to blow dry and get dressed. I came out just when it was time to leave for the bus—now to catch my ride with Oliver—grab a piece of buttered toast from the table and go. Oliver followed me outside, still chewing whatever Jennie had given him. Bacon, a boiled egg, a handful of blueberries. She liked him. And she was telling my dad about him. I knew. Because after Oliver started showing up, my dad started looking at me with a tiny hint of a smile at his lips. His eyes sparkled a bit. I think he thought the bad stuff was over and I was going to move on nicely. And that might have been true. Except that it wasn't.

Oliver parked his car far out, at the edges of the lot at school and we sat, waiting until the last possible moment that we had to get to class. I didn't think Oliver was that type, to be honest. He was the kind who got to class early, traded jokes with the teachers, flirted with the girls, talked sports with the guys. But there he sat every morning since he started driving me to school. And he never said things like, "Are you ready?" or, "Should we go?" He waited. He waited.

That particular morning, he asked me if we could go see a movie on Friday and I told him I didn't think so.

"Why not?"

I shrugged.

"You don't like movies?"

"Not really," I said.

He laughed. "Who doesn't like movies?"

We were quiet for a minute. The vice principal, Mr. Kettering, was walking the perimeter of the parking lot. If you drove into school late, he'd shout at you. If he caught you up against the fence, he'd escort you to the building. He had a pregnant paunch—the buttons on his cotton shirts always stressed—and carried a whistle. We were dogs to him. If he caught Oliver and me still sitting in the car, he'd rap on the window with his knuckles and remind us that it was almost time for classes to start.

"Still," Oliver said, startling me. I turned to face him. "You won't go with me?"

"I don't think it's a good idea."

"It's just a movie."

"Not the movie."

"What then?"

"Us."

He looked around, out his window, into the rear view mirror. Then he put his hands on the steering wheel and stared at them. "Why not?"

"It's just not."

"Look, I don't care, you know. About the hoarding. About your mom." He was talking now to the parking lot ahead of him. "I get that you've got this...broken thing going on—"

"What is that supposed to mean?"

"Honest to God, Lenore." He turned to look at me. "I'm not making light of it. Of you. I'm saying...I'm only trying to say..."

"What?"

"I like you." And then he put his hand on my shoulder, leaned over, and tried to kiss me.

"Oh, my God." I pulled my backpack from the floor and got out of the car.

Oliver followed me, caught up to me. "I'm sorry. Okay, okay," he said. "We don't have to get serious or anything. Just a movie."

"Just a movie," I mimicked.

"Really. I don't want to push you into anything."

I stopped and turned to him. "Why? Why do you like me?"

"Get to class," Mr. Kettering called. I rolled my eyes in his direction. "I'm nothing like you, Oliver," I said. "I'm the complete opposite of every girl you've ever dated."

He smiled a crooked smile. "You know all the girls I've dated?"

"For Christ's sake, Oliver." I walked again, him tagging along like a lost puppy. "Everybody knows every girl you've dated."

"So, you're different. I like different."

We were at the front walk by then and I didn't want to have that conversation in front of anybody else.

"Come on." He grabbed my arm before we had to split up for first class. "Just a movie."

"Okay, fine."

But this thing could only end badly. I tried to tell him that weekend. I thought that if he could understand it, imagine the timeline of it, he would see that my future wasn't going to be anything like his. We were not the only two members of the dead mothers club at Sandy Point High. He was the only member of that club. I was in a whole other lock up.

The house began to fill, I told him. Shopping trips more frequent. Deliveries to the house and boxes opened but not emptied stacked up in corners. I wanted Oliver to feel it. The claustrophobia that would eventually right itself, twist everything around until it all turned the other side up, right becomes left, dark is light, until it's the outside—the wide open, empty rooms and drawers and pages—that feel wrong. Clutter becomes cover. Stacks become soothing friends. Piles—glorious, chaotic, teetering piles—become beloved caresses. The house began to fill and my father spent more and more time away. And when he was home, there was arguing. Shouting. They both threw things. He threw what he called trash into the bins beside the house outside. She threw his clothes on the lawn. And toward the end, she was accusing him of not caring about Will. He hadn't been with us at the beach; it was somehow his fault. He stood it. I can still remember the clench in his jaw as he kept himself to himself. Until that one night, when I sat at the dinner table, too sick with fear to eat—Mom to my left, Dad to my right—their voices grew softer, hushed, sinister, when he told her she had no business going to the beach with two children, alone. It was…a growl, of a sort. A pain that he had to assuage, but he only knew how to do it by hurting her. What was she thinking, anyway? he asked.

She broke. And we moved out the next day.

10.

Everything was fine that morning. Mother in the kitchen frying eggs. Dad straightening his tie in front of the little mirror in the foyer. Her prim smile as he left the house. Then she turned and I could see that she'd been holding something inside. It came out now. Her face twisted in pain, she dug the suitcases out of the garage, dragged them into the house, threw them open on her and Dad's big bed and started throwing clothes into them. I stood, at the edges of her rage, following but not too closely, as she made trip after trip to the car, a Plymouth—a weird turquoise green, stretched out long in the front, same in the back, with a dark, sloped roof. She loaded every square inch of it, stuffed it. First with the suitcases, then with clothes on hangers. Next were books and catalogs, all the knick-knacks from her curio cabinet. In bags, in boxes, in purses. And I followed, back and forth, whispering, too afraid to speak up. Would there be room in the car for me?

There was. I perched on the passenger seat, the floor at my feet filled with bags, as she drove to my grandmother's house across town. She was sobbing and the tires screeched and she turned around. Again, I whispered. What was it? Could I fix it? Back in the driveway at home, she pulled stuff out of the car, left it on the grass in front of the house, ran inside and started carrying out things from Will's room.

"How could I?" she cried, again and again. "How could I forget?"

The car packed once more, we were on our way—those possessions that hadn't made the cut left on our front lawn and the front door standing wide open. We stayed with my grandmother for three days—she wouldn't allow Mother to bring in anything, except for some clothes. Grandma Seally lived in what Mother called "a filthy little place," without a garage, just a carport, and little grass in the yard, mostly dirt. Her neighborhood, behind the shopping center, between the thoroughfare and the railroad tracks, consisted of only two streets. I crossed the tracks to school and back those three days we lived in her house, wondering each time if my mother would still be there when I got home. On the fourth day, I heard the two of them screaming four houses down and I knew we would be leaving.

Someone had broken into the car in the night and taken everything. Every last thing. Will's sports balls—the ones he actually owned and those Mother had bought after he was dead; his lunch box, his wallet, the plastic trophy he won for perfect attendance in second grade. My mother lay curled up in the dirt and sticker bushes out front, at the curb. Grandma stood, hands on her hips, chewing something like she always was, tsking. I don't think Grandma Seally understood that Will was in the car. That all of the best parts of my mother were in there, too. And now they were both gone. I stood on the driveway for an hour, I think, waiting for my mother to get up and when she finally did, she was empty and cold. She took my arm and put me into the car. She went into the house and came back with her purse—no clothes, nothing else. And she drove us over to the Whisper Hills Apartments.

"It's all good," she said, her voice hoarse and raspy from

the screams. "We're starting from scratch. All clean."

I nodded.

The Whisper Hills Apartments consisted of several two-story buildings around a pool. All the front doors faced the parking lot; we were on the first floor. We sat in the car after getting the keys from the landlord until Mother's breathing calmed a bit. She was challenging herself, I think, preparing for the shock. And it was a shock. Opening the door to the empty space felt like a purge, as if the void in the apartment pulled out my insides, pulled everything from me and spilled it into the air where it was sucked up and made into nothing. We both walked around the tiny space—front room, kitchen, and dining area all together inside the door; a mock of a hallway with a closet at the end and two rooms on either side, mine and hers. Hers boasted a sliding glass door, same as the little living room, with a concrete slab jutting out from it. She could lie in bed, when she got one, and watch people in the pool. My bedroom window looked out onto the parking lot. I had to cross the highway and walk down to the entrance of the country club neighborhood to catch the bus to school.

My mother got a job at Pantry Pride as a cashier. She started getting checks from my father in the mail. I visited him at the house every other weekend and was made to relate to my mother every detail of his life. I lied. One day in February, about a year after we moved in and the apartment was filling up nicely, I was in school, third grade at Coquina Elementary, and I was taken out of class and led to the office by an older kid. My mother stood at the counter, a sickly sweet smile on her face. She was decked out in a pillbox hat with a gauzy veil. Posed in her cream-colored pumps, a navy dress with a wide, cream belt, and a cropped, cream jacket, she gripped a pair of gloves in her hand, twisting and wringing at them. She took me to the car and drove.

"Are we going shopping?"

She said nothing. But she drove to the Searstown Mall. I followed her into the store, keeping my distance as she went through the dresses and tops on the racks in the women's clothing section, dragging the hangers along the circular metal tubing that held them, making them screech and echo. She bought dozens of tops and dresses, three pairs of shoes, a waffle iron, a bedspread, four sets of queen-sized sheets, a new vacuum cleaner, four pairs of pierced earrings—I dared not mention her ears were not pierced—and thirty-two pairs of pantyhose. Once we lugged the loot into our apartment, she turned to me standing among the bags in the little living room, panting, and slapped me hard across the face, knocking me onto the bag with the bedspread in it.

"Five months," she screamed, ripping the pillbox from her head, the gauzy veil grabbing on to her hair as she did so, leaving it out of place, as if reaching, as if fleeing her head. "Five months."

I shook my head, held my hand to my cheek. "What?"

Mother reached behind me and took the waffle iron box out of a bag, climbed over the other bags, and the bags from previous shopping trips yet to be unpacked, and went into the kitchen where she slit the plastic tape and opened it, flinging the waffle iron out and onto the counter. I followed, as stealthily as I could, and watched as she yanked at bowls and spatulas, tore ingredients from shelves, floured the kitchen. She was making waffles.

"He's getting married," she yelled. "To that bitch."

I knew the bitch, of course. I'd been out to dinner and the movies with her and Dad. They were getting married and I was supposed to be a flower girl. I was going to wear a white dress—they showed it to me in the catalog—with lace on the hem, white patent leather shoes with a gold clasp, and dainty white socks. I would carry a basket full of white flower petals and drop them on the aisle at St. Gabriel's and

Jennie was going to walk on them as she followed me. I didn't understand this at all. But I was told it was an honor And I really wanted the dress.

11.

We were a few days in; the back yard was filling up, but so far, no one from the city had shown up at my door. Hannah was in the back room now filling trash bags. She'd shove in as much as she could in the small space she had, then drag them down the little chute that was my hallway, through the tunnel that was my home, and out the door. Then she'd go back and forth with stuff, filling the bag completely outside where there was more room to stuff it full. She was fast, and quiet, efficient. She wanted the money. I didn't like to think about what for, but I did, anyway. I imagined she would buy drugs with it, worried she wanted to hurt herself. Something lit up in her eyes—an emptiness or a rage, and I realize that you'd think those two emotions would look strikingly different on a face, but maybe they don't. Anyway, I worried that Mel would blame me for it. She'd know somehow it was my fault; I gave her the money. I considered reneging on the deal in the end, but I wasn't sure I'd be able to take the girl's fury. I'd heard her, in the past, screaming at Mel—about being grounded, about having her privacy invaded, all the usual things teenage girls take seriously. Then I thought maybe she was pregnant and needed an abortion. But who was going to take her? That boyfriend of hers was locked up. I didn't ever see any friends come over to visit her. The girl was alone. What would she want that kind of money for? I settled on the idea that she was going to run away. I thought I could get some truth out of her so I could at least help Mel when the girl turned up missing. But I wasn't good at talking to people—never had been.

I could hear her back there in my room—hear my things sliding and thumping into trash bags—singing to herself, coughing up dust, smacking at bugs, occasionally swearing. When I heard the mountain collapse I jumped up from the sofa and tripped over piles of magazines trying to get to the hallway.

"Hannah?"

She didn't answer me.

"Hannah!" I snaked my way down the hall, my heart pounding. Everything seemed to go black. I couldn't breathe. Trembling, I let out a gasp and stopped in the hall, my arms holding me steady between the wall and a stack of boxes. I could see my mother on the floor of our apartment, looking up at me. My knees buckled. Then I heard Hannah weeping.

"Hannah," I said. Making my way to the doorway, I found her sitting on a pile of clothes and books. She looked at me, a helplessness in her face that tore me up. "What is it? What's wrong?" I looked around at my old bedroom, what I could see of it. She'd cleared away quite a lot, but I still couldn't find the bed or the dressers. Part of one closet door behind the girl was exposed, but the other half still hidden behind piles of bags and boxes. She was so small, surrounded by a mountain of...junk.

Hannah climbed to her feet, balanced on the uneven mounds covering the floor, and wiped her hands off on her pants. "This will never work," she said, still crying. "I'll never find a small box in this mess."

We stood looking at each other for a few seconds, until

I shook my head. "It's okay."

"It is not."

"I don't blame you. This is my fault. Hell, it'd serve me right to die without it."

I turned and made my way back down the hallway. I thought she'd follow me, but instead, I heard her grunting, wheezing. She was attacking the hoard, throwing stuff into a bag as if it was all evil.

"I mean it," I called to her. "I don't care, anymore."

She made a few more trips out to the back yard, crying harder each time.

"Just stop," I finally told her from the sofa when she stomped in from outside. "No more. Let me let it go. Let me come to terms with it."

She glared at me, wiped her face with both her hands. "You said you'd pay me five hundred dollars."

"What do you want with five hundred dollars, anyway?"

"None of your business."

"And like you said, how are you even going to find it? Hell, I ain't even sure it's in that room."

"What?" She fell—her eyes, her chin, her shoulders. "But you said—"

"I know what I said. Forget it."

"No."

She went back to work, determination fighting tears. I heard her scream, finally, and another crash. She appeared in front of me, angry. Her face red and splotchy from crying. "You are a fucking weirdo," she yelled. "Can't you smell this place? You're breathing in all this dust. Don't you see it? You've got flies for God's sake. What is wrong with you?"

I raised my brows. "Is that it? Is that the best you got?"

"Fine," she said, seething. "Forget the whole God damned thing."

She turned and left. I heard the door slam, and then the screen door pop back into place, and the house was quiet.

That full, anticipatory quiet—waiting for more. There was no more. Nothing fell, nothing slid, no avalanche to mark her dramatic exit. I grabbed at the remote and turned the volume back up on the television. *Family Feud*. That new host I didn't like. I sat staring at the opening to my cocoon, expecting her to come back. To do what? To apologize? What for? To get back to work? I chuckled to myself. Again, what for? She was right. Hannah was smarter than I was. Maybe I hadn't really expected her to find it. Maybe I just wanted some company while I died. And how sick was that? At some point, the sky outside darkened and I hadn't bothered to turn on the lamp that was perched on the boxes next to my spot. I startled, as if I'd been asleep, and there she was, standing in front of me looking full up, ready to spring into life.

"She's not my mother," she said.

12.

My mother was supposed to pick me up at the church after the wedding. My father and Jennie were gone, the guests were gone, the priest was gone. It was Jennie's mother who waited with me outside, on the steps. She was telling me that she was now my grandmother, and I could call her grandma, or granny, ever Charlotte, if I preferred. We sat. I had my knees up to my chin, tapping my feet on the concrete, imagining my new white patent leather shoes had metal taps on the toes. Jennie had put a curling iron to my head and sprayed my hair until it crackled. I had a smart white hat with a lacy brim Someone, I'd no idea who in the rush of women getting ready for the wedding, had pinned it onto my head. Now it was teetering with every move I made. My curls had gone flat. A grass stain covered one of my knees—I'd been allowed to run around the church a few times with the other children after the ceremony, to burn off our energy we were told, and I'd fallen.

"We're all so sorry your mother wouldn't allow you to go to the reception," she said.

Charlotte had her knees together, her legs bent sideways. She'd taken her shoes off—said it was better to snag her pantyhose than to scuff up her best pumps. When I look back on it, I can't remember Charlotte's face. She died soon after that, before I ever saw her again. I always put Betty White's face on her when I remember her. I think it's because of *The Mary Tyler Moore Show* and that sickly sweet, yet snide smile of her character, Sue Ann something. When my mother proved a no-show, Charlotte's sweetness took a dive and she begrudgingly drove me home, dropped me off in front of our apartment, and wished me luck.

The apartment was locked. I knocked on the door, again and again. I walked around the building to see if Mother was out by the pool; she wasn't. Her car was in our space, in front of the door; she had to be home. I knocked on the sliding glass door in the back. I knocked on sliding door at her bedroom. I called to her. Nothing. Back at the front door, I knocked again. I heard something inside. My mother's voice. She was angry. I tried the door again and it was unlocked, so I went in.

My mother was on the sofa, surrounded by shopping bags. But she wasn't excited. She wasn't taking stuff out, showing it off. She sat and stared at the wall across the room; and she rocked slightly side to side.

"Mom?"

She looked at me and blinked slowly. "Go to bed," she said. "And take off that get up."

"But it's not even dark."

She leapt from the sofa and slapped me hard across the face. Grabbing my forearm, she dragged me down the little hallway and shoved me into my room. "You stay in there and don't come out until morning," she said. "And take off that dress and those shoes. Filthy little witch." She stood in the doorway watching me. "Now!"

I did as I was told and handed her the shoes and the dress and the little hat Jennie had bought for me. She took them and slammed my door shut, leaving me in there crying.

I heard her leave the apartment—peered out the window as she got in her car and drove away. I didn't dare leave my room even knowing she was gone. I found my pajamas and curled up in bed, waiting for night to come. When I woke up, it was dark. I heard her at her bedroom door. She was laughing, whispering loudly—her voice was hoarse and off key. Then I heard a man's voice and her door closed.

My mother found a new level of crazy after my father's wedding. She found excuses, too, for why I couldn't go visit him on the weekends that I was supposed to. Sometimes he persisted, at least at first, but when Jennie turned up pregnant, he gave up trying. I couldn't blame him, not now anyway, looking back on it. If he came to get me, my mother would hurl insults, curses, and sometimes objects at him. If she dropped me off, she came to his door and screamed at him and Jennie. It was better for him to leave me with her. And anyway, I don't think he realized what she was doing. He just kept sending money—more and more of it. And she kept spending it.

The apartment filled up quickly—with stuff and people and ashtrays and liquor. At first, I was always sent into my room. I'd stuff a towel against the bottom of my door trying to keep out the cigarette smoke. But by the time I was thirteen, I'd been smoking myself for three years, and I was allowed to join the party after Mom had a few drinks in her.

I told Oliver this—right up to the part about Rob Calloway—at the point where I should have mentioned his name.

We were at the Burger King on U.S. 1, sitting in one those smooth, curved booths across from each other, eating Whoppers and French fries. He chewed and swallowed and said, "What?"

"What, what?" I said.

"You stopped. Is that it? That's the end of the story? You got to hang out with your mom at adult parties when you were a teenager? That's it?"

"I didn't realize I was telling stories."

He nodded and shoved a bouquet of fries into his mouth. "Fair enough," he mumbled while chewing.

"Why did I even start talking about it?"

"I asked you if you smoked when we were in middle school. I thought you did."

I remembered then. Oliver knew I wanted to tell him something. He'd known it all along. That was why he showed up on the seat next to me on the bus that day. That was why he drove me to school, and why he took me out. He knew somehow there was something inside me that needed to be let out. For a moment, I imagined the police sent him in, undercover; perhaps he was wearing a tiny microphone, recording me. It didn't matter. If I could get that far—if I could put it in words, it would mean it was true and then I'd deserve whatever I got.

"So, go on," he said.

I shook my head.

"It's bad?"

My cheeks burned hot and I had to put my sandwich down. I turned to look around the restaurant. It was two in the afternoon and only seven other booths were taken. Nobody paid us any mind. But I still felt exposed. "It was Rob Calloway."

"Rob Calloway? From those commercials?" He chuckled and mimicked him. "I'll do anything, anything, to sell you a car!" He looked at me, grinning like he'd just found a gold coin. "The guy who got himself shot out of a cannon?"

"That's the one," I said.

"Is he even still alive?"

I imagined myself, as I'd done a million times, stabbing at Rob Calloway with the big carving knife out of one of my mother's knife blocks. "No," I said. "He died a while back." Not that his dying helped at all. That's the sick thing about death—you can wish somebody dead, you can even kill him, but it doesn't help, like you think it will.

"What about him?" Oliver asked.

I shrugged. "I was thirteen," I said.

13.

I stared at Hannah for a few moments, realizing finally that she needed me to help her speak. I understood that feeling. Years and years of having a story to tell and no one willing to listen—it's like swallowing cement while it's pliable only to let it harden in your throat. It takes a lot of chipping away to get at those words and too few people are willing to do the work. I told her to sit—got up to toss all that crap from the other side of the sofa onto the pile on the other side of coffee table so she wouldn't have to perch on the edge like usual. She sank into the cushions and wrapped her arms around herself.

"Go on then," I told her. "What's this all about?"

"She's not my mother," she said again. She'd been crying, I could tell. Her voice was hollow and her eyelids puffed up.

"Who's not?"

"Mel." She was irritated—a good thing. It helps to get the bad stuff out if you spit it. "She's my grandmother."

"Well, that makes some things come into focus, don't it?" Now that I thought about it, Mel was old for having a teenager in the house, my age really—not that that was proof of anything. "She your mother's mother? Or your father's mother?"

"Mother's."

"And where's your mother, then? She dead?"

Hannah shook her head and chewed on a thumbnail, nervous. "Mel says she couldn't take care of me. She took me away from her." She reached up and pulled at her hair, twisted a lock and dragged it across her lips.

"How old were you?"

She shrugged. "Three. I think."

"You see her now and then, though."

"I haven't seen her since." She put her face in her hands, clawing at her forehead, before she looked at me— red lines impressed on her skin above her eyes. "My grandmother stole me from my mother and won't let me see her."

"Stole's a harsh word. You know that for sure?"

"She used to tell me it was for the best. She said my mother was a drug addict; she couldn't help it. Said she'd write to me if she could, or visit. But she can't."

"You don't believe her?"

"Would you?"

I sighed and looked around my hovel at all the strange little things sticking out from the piles—bookmarks, shoelaces, a ruler, the legs of a Barbie doll. I caught sight of a bit of blue blanket—I'd searched and searched for that last winter when we had a day or two of cold weather and couldn't find it. And there it was all along. Not that I could have gotten to it. If I'd pulled at that little corner poking out from under those three awkwardly stacked boxes, the whole thing could have come down. I wondered, then...did I actually find it last winter and forget?

"I suppose I wouldn't," I told Hannah. And it was probably the truth. I was a distrustful person by nature. "But sometimes the truth is worse than the lie."

"What could be worse than being stolen?"

"She hasn't ever tried to get to you? Call you or nothing?"

"Mel won't let her!" She leaned forward a bit, as if to get up, then seemed to think better of it and let herself fall back into the sofa. "I bet if I looked in Mel's closet, I could find cards and letters she's written to me. Mel would keep me from seeing them."

"Have you ever found anything like that?"

"No, but that doesn't mean I couldn't."

"I'm just saying..."

"Well, don't I have the right to know either way? If my mom doesn't want me, or can't take care of me...she should tell me herself. Right?"

The desperation in her voice was off somehow. I couldn't read it correctly. But I understood how hard it could be to confess something shameful to a stranger. "So, what is it you want the five-hundred dollars for?" I asked her. "You thinking of finding your mom?"

"I found her address in Mel's personal notebook—"

"Snooping? That ain't right. That never turns out right."

"I don't care. I found it. Now I need bus fare and enough for a hotel and food."

"Where is it she's at?" I was thinking of a bus trip across the country, and how dangerous that could be.

"Tampa," she said.

And before I could even think, I was saying, "Tampa? Why hell, I can take you to Tampa."

She looked like I'd stunned her, slapped her. "You'd do that?"

"Well..." I had to consider the whole thing. "I didn't mean I would. Just that I could. It's not so far. But, well, I don't know about a trip."

She rolled her eyes. "Never mind. I can get there by myself. I'll get Nicky to take me."

"You said he was locked up."

"Not forever."

"Are you sure you want to do that? You and him alone

on the road."

"Well, it's that or the bus on my own."

"I bet if you asked, Mel would take you to see her."

"You don't think I've asked her? She told me a long time ago that I couldn't see her. She said something about the law, that I wasn't allowed."

"Then you'd better not do it, don't you think?"

"Oh, come on. You don't believe that shit, do you?"

"You don't have to cuss about it."

"She lied to me. I know she lied. She just doesn't want me to find my mother, because she knows my mother will want me to stay with her."

"Sure, I guess," I said. "But she's probably right about the law. I mean, if she's got custody of you, and maybe there's something that says your mother isn't allowed to see you..."

"That's impossible," she stood up now, and made her way toward the hall. "What court would do that?"

"If your mom is a drug addict."

"That was ten years ago."

"I'm not arguing." Both of our voices had raised, seemed to startle the boxes surrounding us, made me feel like they were closing in further, trying to shut us up.

"I don't care," she said, quieter now. "I'm going to see my mother." She stared at me for a few seconds, daring me to say anything against the idea. "Will you still give me the money if I find your box, or not?"

I nodded. "I'll give it to you."

"Don't tell Mel."

"Well, now, I don't know."

"If you tell her, she won't let me find your box."

"I told you," I said, "I don't care anymore."

She smiled—a bit. A sly, teasing sort of look. "We both know that's not true."

It was then I realized she was a lot older than I'd given

her credit for. She knew a lot more than I thought she did. And that worried me—something that also pricked at me. Why was I worrying about this girl? I wondered if it was because she's so much like me—stubborn, and willful, and with stories to tell. But not too much, I hoped. Not too much.

14.

I expected more of a reaction from Oliver. I'm ashamed now to confess it. When I look back on it, I wonder if I wasn't simply trying to shock him—make him think twice about getting mixed up with me. How much of it was me trying to scare him away? As much as I tried to convince myself at the time that I only needed to tell somebody—just needed the words to leave my body and dissipate into the air around me—I think the truth of it was much worse. I think I wanted to be caught.

He sat back and nodded. "I think I might have heard something about that."

"What?"

"Yeah," he said. "Did you...I mean...I don't know how to put this. Did you get...?"

"Pregnant?"

"Yeah."

"Not by Rob Calloway," I said. "Are you telling me that people were talking about me being pregnant?"

He blushed and offered me a sheepish grin. "There was a rumor."

I chuckled. "How do people find these things out?"

"So you were? I mean...you did...have an...?"

"Abortion?"

He let out a sigh of relief, like he couldn't get at the gist of it himself. "Yes."

"I did. But that was last year."

"Oh." He seemed disappointed. "But you and this Calloway guy?"

"He was a man," I said. "Like, forty years old. And I was thirteen."

"Did he go to jail?"

Here I laughed. "Hardly."

"Was it...?"

"Rape?"

He nodded.

"What do you think?"

"I'm sorry," he said. "I didn't mean to imply...I just meant..."

"It's okay. I know what you meant. It wasn't knock down, drag out, jump out from the bushes rape."

"He got you drunk."

"Several times. Things progressed. Further and further. Until we were in my bedroom."

He was staring at me, frowning.

"Don't ask me if I tried to fight him," I said. "Don't ask me if I said no or anything. It doesn't work like that, you know? It's not like you understand what's happening—not like you don't even want it to happen. I don't even understand it myself."

He lowered his gaze to the table, at his half eaten hamburger, his fries soaked in ketchup; it looked as if he was going to cry. "I'm sorry," he mumbled.

"I'm not telling you this so you'll feel sorry for me."

He looked up now, concerned. "No, I know that. Maybe you need to talk about it."

"I just need somebody to know."

"Sure," he nodded.

"And I don't need you to do anything with it. I mean, you don't have to tell anybody, or remember it even. I just ...need someone to have known about it." I rolled my eyes and took a bite of my burger.

"No, I get it," he said. "You can tell me anything, Lenore. Seriously, anything. I'm your guy."

I didn't believe him.

When Oliver took me to the dance, put on by this club he was in—Key Club, something like that—he drove us there in silence. I thought he might be angry; but I'd never known Oliver to be mad at anybody. As it turns out, he was only giving me another space, a really long one, in which to tell him something. But I didn't. The problem with car rides is that they end. And you might not be finished with the telling. Then you're left sitting in a parked car finishing up. There's too much anticipation left in that—too much hurrying to get to the punchline.

The dance was held in the Knights of Columbus building up north of town. It was a square of concrete blocks, like a Lego house, with no windows, dark and hot. I felt as if everyone was watching us as Oliver paid for two tickets and we got the backs of our hands stamped. Inside, it was bodies and strobe lights; a huge disco ball hung from the ceiling over the dance floor, turning slowly, reflecting colorful lights all over the place. We danced until we were wet, Oliver smiling. The thing about Oliver, I think, is that he didn't care what anyone thought about him. For a long time, I figured that was wrong. After all, my mother invested a lot of time and energy in hiding who she was.

After Rob Calloway, she stopped having people over and the apartment filled quickly with all the things she needed to forget about the whole incident. When the eviction notice came—taped onto the front door for everyone in the building to see—she raged, threw things, called the landlord, cursed him, told him, "How dare you enter my apartment without permission?" I don't know what the landlord said, but we moved out soon after. My father helped her buy a house mid-town. I could walk to school then and I liked that. I felt free, somehow. You don't feel trapped at school when home is only a mile away.

But apartments are public. People everywhere all the time. Next door, you can hear them through the thin walls and know they're probably listening to you when you're shouting, too. Outside your door, there they are. People coming and going. Some of them are friendly. They ask questions. They see when you come home and when you leave and who you're with. They see the bags of groceries and what's inside them when they try to help you carry them inside. And they glimpse all the stuff just beyond the front door.

Houses? They can be very private. Everyone keeps a respectable distance. There's not so much need for conversation when you have to cross a lawn or two to engage in it. People keep more to themselves. What goes on inside your house is your own business.

The music slowed and before I could turn to leave the dance floor, Oliver pulled me close to him, pressed our bodies together. What little light there had been was dimmed. He put his hand to my neck, lifted my face to his and kissed me—deep, slowly, hungry. Then, with our foreheads together, he said, "I know what you're doing."

"What?" I asked him.

"Telling me stories, trying to get me to go away. I'm not going anywhere. No matter what you say."

I wanted to ask him why. I wanted to know how far I would have to go to get him to realize that I was not what he thought I was—I was not right. Not for him. Not for the world. But instead, I let him kiss me until the song was over.

15.

Rob Calloway was forty-something, and balding. He wore bell bottomed jeans, platform shoes, and silk shirts unbuttoned to the waist—gold chains hung around his neck. Crosses and skulls. They tangled with his thick curly chest hairs. I used to stare at the shiny gold charms, barely able to resist the urge to tug on them, rip out the hair they clung to, see what he'd do. The hair on his head was much darker than that on his chest. I was pretty sure he dyed it. And he sprayed it fanatically in our little bathroom behind the kitchen. I had reason to suspect him of flossing his teeth in there whenever he came over.

I always knew when company was coming. My mother would race around picking up piles of her stuff and tossing them into her room, behind her bed, beside her dresser, onto the floor in the closet. She never got it all, of course, but managed to make it look as if she and I were merely messy people, busy people, people who led interesting lives and hadn't the time for something as banal as housekeeping. I doubt her friends noticed or cared. They came to listen to the music, cook out on the grill on our little slab of a back porch, drink, and smoke pot. There seemed to be an unspoken agreement with the residents of building C. The police were never called. No one banged on the wall or yelled for us to keep quiet. Most likely, the neighbors joined the party as it spilled out into the courtyard, by the pool.

I was thirteen, then. Bored. Angry. My mother had finally allowed me to spend time with my father, but I hated his house. What I'd imagined all those years as a place of solace had turned out to be a museum. Jennie kept trinkets in a cabinet, behind glass. Space was left between each one —too much space. When she took me, David, and little Paige to the mall, she'd stop by the housewares departments, or tour the gift shops, run her fingers over little statues of cutesy children and glass figurines so delicate it seemed a mere touch would shatter them. But she didn't buy them. She didn't bring home bags and boxes full of them and struggle to find room for them in her curio cabinet.

"Don't you want it?" I asked her once as she cradled a tiny ceramic owl.

She sighed. "Yes and no."

That made no sense to me. "If you want it, buy it. It's not like you can't afford it."

She glared at me. "That's just it, Len. Your dad works hard so I can stay home with your brother and sister. Don't touch that, Paige." She swatted gently at the girl's hand as it reached for the shelf of statues. "And he supports you and your mother."

"Mom works." I ignored the way she always called David and Paige my brother and sister. Jennie wished we were all a real family. She wished my mother didn't exist. I understood that feeling very well. But I couldn't give her any satisfaction by admitting it.

"Your father helps her a lot. We shouldn't be talking about this."

"I'm not a little girl. I know what's going on."

"Still."

"So, buy it."

She put the owl carefully back on the shelf, took Paige's hand, and led us out of the stuffy, cramped store, into the cool air of the mall. "You don't just buy everything you want."

I never understood that. My mother made more sense to me. The buying part, at least. The act of bringing it home and looking at it, treasuring it. But my mother didn't display the things she bought. She put them back into the bags and stored them under her bed, under the table, next to the sofa. She didn't want anyone to know what she'd done. Especially when people came over. It was as if she suddenly saw our apartment from a new perspective. She realized there were piles of junk in the corners and on the tables. Reality came to the fore and she had to hide it.

I was always sent to my room when the doorbell rang the first time. The year I met Rob Calloway, I'd started waiting an hour or two, let my mother have a few drinks in her, before coming out of my room. I'd wander through the maze of adults sneaking snacks from the trays of goodies my mom and her friends laid out. Cheeses and crackers. Candies. Veggie trays with Ranch dressing for dip. One time, someone brought a layered sandwich—tuna salad, chicken salad, egg salad, pimiento cheese—iced with a slathering of cream cheese. I ate half of it while the rest of the party danced and gossiped. I met him over a plate of pigs in blankets on a Saturday night.

He smiled. "I don't think we've met," he said.

"We haven't."

He held out his hand and we shook, like business partners. "Rob," he said

"Lenore."

"You don't have a drink."

I shook my head.

"Let me fix that."

I stuffed my mouth with the pigs in blankets while watching him in the kitchen pouring liquor into cups. He carried them back to the dining room table, elbowing his way through the crowd, and handed me one.

"Long Island Iced Tea," he said with a wink.

I'd never had an alcoholic drink before, but I'd been high off the fumes of my mother's parties so I didn't imagine it could be much different. Still, with that first sip, and the few after, I felt a warmth travel down my body, weakening my knees. Rob Calloway was there to lean on. When I look back on it, I see it differently. At the time, I thought I was grown up. I thought I was accepted. Because when Rob and I would dance and his hand would roam up and down my back, or when he would pull me onto his lap when he sat on the sofa, bounce me on his knee. I thought I was just another girl at the party and I was glad that my mother didn't mind. But I can see it now, from far away—I see the way I glanced at her now and then...waiting for her to intervene, to stop the inevitable. And I can feel my hatred, boiling in my chest. I hear myself screaming.

It took Rob Calloway three weeks to get to my bedroom door. Another week to kiss me on the lips. And another before he was in my room, tucking me into bed, sitting beside me, curling my hair behind my ear, whispering a goodnight. The week after that, there was no goodnight. I was very drunk, much more so than ever before. He must have known that. He helped me get undressed and when I pointed to the foot of the bed where my nightgown lay, he shook his head and pulled the cover back on the bed.

"You won't need that tonight," he said.

He took off my bra and pushed me gently onto the bed, lifted my legs, lay me down. I remember being somewhat surprised when he crawled in beside me. Afraid, when he slid his hands inside my underwear. And then, as if there were a strict and unyielding line drawn between slow and frantic, he was on top of me, forcing his way inside me and I was crying. It lasted too long. I'd gone numb—gone someplace else in my mind.

When he rolled off me, he chuckled. "That wasn't so bad, for the first time, was it?" he said.

I shook my head, quick little jerks, wishing he would go away.

He propped himself up on one elbow to look down at me. "It'll be better next time. Honest. It always is."

Leaning in, he planted little wet kisses all over my face, one hand cupped over my left breast, the thumb playing with the nipple. Something happened to me. Something wrong.

16.

Hannah cleaned out the back bedroom, bit by bit, until she'd managed to get to the edge of the big bed and one side of the dresser. She worked faster now, determined. I watched as she hauled out bag after bag full of my stuff, sweating, sometimes humming. Telling me about her plans, I imagined, made it all seem possible for her. But I couldn't help thinking there was something off about the whole thing. Maybe I was wrong, but it seemed to me that if Mel took her away from her own mother, there had to be a reason. But I supposed that Hannah deserved to know about it.

One day, later that week, she called out, "I found it." Coming down the hall, she said it again. "I found the box. Is this it?"

I was sitting on the edge of the sofa, stunned. I had no idea I'd lost faith—given up. She held out the small box so I could see the top of it. There, etched in black against the enameled pine was the rock and beneath it, the words: Chimney Rock Park. My heart fluttered and I nodded, reaching for it. She came around the coffee table and placed the box in my trembling hands and I just stared at it.

"Go on," she said. "Open it."

I shook my head, but not meaning to.

"You want me to leave? I can leave."

"No," I whispered. "Stay. I'll...I'll open it."

I pulled at the little metal latch and, sucking in a deep breath, lifted the lid. It was empty. We both sat silent for a moment before I managed to lift my eyes from the box and sigh.

"It's okay," she said. "I can find it; if you tell me what it is you're looking for."

"An envelope. Addressed to a friend of mine. It was stamped, sealed, ready to mail."

"You wanted to mail it, before you..."

"I don't know. Maybe. It's no use now."

"No." An edge of desperation rang in her voice. "I can find it." She stood and stepped over my junk making her way to the hall.

"It's no use," I said. "You might have already found it—tossed it into a bag."

"Then I'll look through all the bags. Who is it addressed to? What am I looking for exactly?"

"You don't have to—"

"I need that five hundred dollars, Mrs. Hawn. Please."

"Of course, of course," I said. "Oliver Stanton. In South Carolina."

She smiled, relieved. "I'll find it; I promise."

I didn't have the heart to refuse the girl. But I was already trying to make myself let it go. I couldn't remember why I'd had the idea at all—must have been the shock of death reaching out for me so quickly. I couldn't actually mail it. Paige had sent me the address; she got it from Oliver's brother. Oliver was living up in Columbia, a doctor in a pediatrics clinic. She said he wasn't married—no doubt she had the bizarre idea that I could have a life with him—but that was twenty years ago. He'd no doubt settled down by now—had a family. Not that I'd written anything that would make him think I wanted him. Still. It was too late. He didn't need to know. Nobody needed to know, now. Not ever. I didn't have to tell.

The next day, Mel showed up just after lunchtime. I heard her calling from the back door. "Mrs. Hawn? Can I come in?"

I told her to come on through and she met Hannah at the entrance to my little front room.

"What's going on? The neighbors sent me over. Said you had Hannah filling up your back yard with stuff."

I laughed. "They didn't say 'stuff' did they?"

"Does it matter?" She grimaced, embarrassed. "They're going to call the city again. But they asked me to tell you first."

Hannah was looking at me, fearful.

"I asked her to find something for me is all," I said. "We'll have the stuff back inside in no time."

Mel shook her head. "I don't think they'll accept that. I'm sorry."

"You don't have to apologize."

"Can't you just tell them?" Hannah said.

"You don't understand," Mel said. "This happened before. By law, Mrs. Hawn has to keep her stuff out of her yard."

"But it's only bags."

"Hannah, it's a mess out there. The city will fine Mrs. Hawn."

"But we'll bring it back in."

"Well, it's likely the city will take a while to get out here. And then you'll have thirty days."

"No," I said. "I've been in too much trouble over this before. If they come out, I could go to jail.'

"Jail?" Hannah said. "They can't do that."

"Don't shout," Mel said. "Just put the stuff back inside. I'll help. And I'll tell the neighbors we'll have it all back in within a day or two. My God—" she turned toward the back of the house— "you must have dumped a hundred bags out there."

"But," Hannah looked at me, helpless.

"I told you," I said quietly so Mel wouldn't hear me. "It ain't in the cards, honey." I could see all the hope she had for seeing her mother fall away; tears welled up in her eyes. "I'm sorry."

I don't know how she managed to get herself together before she got outside to help Mel carry the bags in. Anger, I imagined. I tried to help, but Mel insisted I sit still and watch television while they did all the heavy lifting. People have this idea that when you're dying, you want to prolong it for as long as possible. As if sitting in my little cocoon, the cats hiding somewhere in the hoard, watching my tinny sounding television set was worth a few more days of living. And maybe it worked that way for people like Mel. Maybe the longer they could stay alive, thinking, remembering, the more joy they could eke out before that dark expanse of nothingness. It doesn't work that way for the rest of us. And then it hit me—just like that. I did have something to live for.

As Hannah passed the front room on her way back outside for another bag, I stopped her, waved her over, closer. "I'll take you over to Tampa, myself," I said. There had to be a happy ending somewhere, for somebody.

17.

I thought my mother knew about Rob Calloway. I hated her for it. Even when I realized she hadn't known at all, I still hated her. In my ignorant, thirteen-year-old mind, Rob Calloway was my boyfriend. He never called, never took me anywhere; but I had it in my head that he loved me. What I felt for him was not so easily understood. Each morning after he'd been in my bed, I was sickened by him, disgusted. All I could remember was the crudity of it: stickiness, the odor of sex, the things he made me look at, touch. I took long, very hot showers, breathing in the steam, glad that my mother was too hungover to care. But as the day would wear on, I would find myself feverish. Quiet moans would escape me when I remembered what he'd done; my breath would quicken and I'd have to find a dark, hidden place—my room, the girl's bathroom stall at school —and find release. And then I wanted him in my bed again.

The days of waiting for my mother to signal that her friends were coming to the apartment were agony. But not physically, no. After the initial shock of it wore off each time, after the fever left me, I would be confused, not sure if I really liked him at all. He reeked of strong cologne, cigarettes, and rum. His hands were rough and calloused.

His eyes were almost yellow, as if he were a demon. His skin was browned like leather and his nose had a bulb at the tip of it. He sometimes forced himself into my mouth—yanked at my hair and pinched me when he came. That couldn't be love, I reasoned. But I was also worried, wondering if I had it right. Was he my boyfriend? Were we dating? Did he not call me because he knew he was too old for me? Was I being used?

When my mother would start her ritual of frantic tidying up, fear would grip me. I'd grab a tall glass of ice and lock myself in my bedroom—I'd hidden a bottle of rum and cans of Coke in my closet—and drink, telling myself I wouldn't come out this time. And I wouldn't let him in if he tried, even if he begged. But by the time her friends started showing up, I was changed, sure that I was much older than I looked in the mirror. I could handle Rob Calloway. I'd dress and make up my face and leave my room in search of him. As soon as he caught my eye in the smoky crowd of people, he'd call out to me, welcome me into the party as if I belonged there. And nobody ever said a word against it.

I tried to tell Oliver this, but the words wouldn't come. Some details I'd just have to keep to myself, I supposed.

Oliver and I were officially dating, according to the rules of the upper echelons of Sandy Point High School society. I knew, by the looks and the whispers and rolling eyes, that we were an enigma to them. Why had Oliver Stanton sunk so low? I couldn't tell them; I had no idea myself.

We were up in the stands, top row, in the gym, at spring assembly. The orchestra was set up on one end of the gym floor and across from them, under the other basketball goal, sat rows and rows of teachers. Speeches were ignored and announcements chuckled at; eyes rolled at talent displays. Oliver was watching the whole thing, quiet, reserved, when he suddenly turned to me, leaned in so I could hear him and asked, "How did it end? With that Calloway guy?"

I didn't like to remember that part. It was summer. My birthday was on a Saturday. My mother had promised me a shopping trip a month before, but she left that morning for work without mentioning it. I walked down Park Avenue to the convenience store and bought a Snickers bar and a bottle of Coke and sat at the edge of the parking lot. After I'd had a few bites, I heard something behind me and when I turned, a bearded man wearing dirty pants and a button up plaid shirt that hung in rags from his shoulders shuffled toward me in torn sneakers. He'd come from the back of the building.

"Got anything to spare?" he asked me.

I nodded and dug out some bills from my purse. I was finished with the Snickers bar when he came out of the store with a six-pack of beer. He sat beside me and lit up a cigarette, offering me one. I took it and used his matchbook to light it.

"Thanks for the cash," he said. "You live around here?"

"Down the road."

"Summer," he said.

I nodded.

"Hot as hell."

The cigarette wasn't menthol; at first it was harsh, but after a few drags, I started to like it. There was something hard and real about it, as if menthols were for girls. Roo Calloway smoked menthols.

"How old are you? If you don't mind me asking," he said.

"Why would I mind?"

He chuckled. "I'm not so old that I can't remember adults always nagging us about stupid stuff. How old are you? When you gonna be eighteen? What's your favorite class in school? It's like adults don't know how to relate at all. And yet, we've been where you are. We just can't remember for some reason."

I smiled at him and nodded. "It would hurt too much to remember," I said.

He sucked in a long toke and blew the smoke out of his nose. "I think you got that right."

"How old are *you*?" I asked him.

"Fair enough. Twenty-three."

"That's not old."

"Bet I look older."

"A little. I'm fourteen. Today."

"It's your birthday?"

I nodded, but I'd lost my smile.

"What have you got planned?"

"Nothing. My mom has to work."

"Where are your friends?"

"I don't have friends."

He looked at me warily. "Pretty girl like you?"

I shrugged.

"I didn't mean that," he said. "You don't have to be pretty to have friends. There's got to be some kids in your neighborhood."

"I know some kids at school," I said, almost apologizing. "I don't like most of them."

"You're too mature for them, I bet." He winked at me.

"Maybe."

We sat and smoked and I thought about it—thought about the truth of it, which was that I just didn't have friends. I'd never had friends. I used to watch other girls talking and playing together at school and it seemed so unnatural, forced and fake. I never even tried it. When someone asked me something, I answered. When they said something, I nodded. Then they'd turn around and talk to someone else. Whatever it was that I was supposed to do to make friends was lost on me.

"What's your name?" the man said.

"Lenore. What's yours?"

"Well, birthday girl, Lenore, I'm Benny." He popped open one of his beers and handed it to me. "Allow me to offer you your first alcoholic beverage."

I took it, smiling, and said, "I think that's for when you turn eighteen."

"I had mine at fourteen. Passing on the legacy."

We clinked cans together and drank. He watched me, suspicious, I think. I'd taken the beer too easily—didn't shudder and wince the way I had the first time I tasted it. I didn't care; I didn't have to pretend.

"Where do you live?" I asked him.

He nodded his head toward the woods behind the store "It's temporary."

"You live back there? In an empty lot?"

"You'd be surprised how many people live in the woods."

When I left him, he told me I could come see him anytime, there in the woods. On the short walk back to the apartment, I wondered if I looked like I needed help. Was there something about my face, or in my eyes, that pleaded with people? I stared at myself for a while that afternoon, in the mirror over the sink in our little bathroom. I practiced expressions—happy, sad, desperate, angry, blank. Blank seemed to come as naturally as any of the others.

That night, Rob Calloway was on top of me in my bed when my mother opened the door and came into my room She flicked on the lights and stood watching us, her face bland and dull.

Rob jumped off me and started getting dressed, cursing "Didn't you lock the door? What were you thinking?" I didn't know if he was talking to me or himself. He stood in front of my mother with a shoe in each hand. "This isn't what it looks like." I swear to God, that's what he said.

My mom glared at him, weaving a bit. She blinked slowly. After Rob Calloway left my room, and we heard the front door slam, she turned and walked out. The next morning, Sunday, I came out of my bedroom into the little dining room at the front door. My mother was at the table, eating eggs and bacon, turning pages in her newspaper. I got a bowl of cereal and sat opposite her.

"I guess Rob thinks he's had quite an adventure," she said without looking up from the paper. "The mother and the daughter."

I froze, mid spoonful. I'd had no idea.

"He'll be telling that story all over town."

I dropped the spoon back into the bowl, no longer hungry.

"Let's hope he makes you eighteen when he tells it; we don't want him arrested, after all. That would be quite the scene." Her voice was unusually deep, with a hard edge to it, as if she'd smoked an entire pack of cigarettes in just an hour.

"Yesterday was my birthday." I sounded like a three-year-old.

Now she looked at me, an angry smile at her lips. "And that was your present, was it?"

"No more than the first time." I wanted to hurt her, and from the look on her face, I'd done it.

"How long?"

I shrugged. "Almost a year." I went back to eating—let her watch me for a while, until she'd had enough.

"You've turned out wild, haven't you?" she said.

"You just now noticed?"

She tossed the newspaper to the floor, got out of her chair and went to her room, slamming the door behind her. Her shopping binges doubled. She'd go out two or three times in a day, bringing home nonsense. She had to have a sewing machine and an ironing board and stacks and stacks of fabrics. She bought bags of yarn. And when she got past the crafting phase, she started in on the idea of having a pet.

Books on dogs and cats and rodents showed up. She subscribed to *Cat Fancy* and *Dog Fancy*. She bought all the necessary paraphernalia for puppy ownership: pee pads, chew toys, leashes, and food bowls. But the eviction notice was on the door before she got the chance to bring a dog home. Before I'd come to terms with whatever it was that had happened with Rob Calloway, she was packing up all of our stuff with boxes she'd got from the grocery store dumpster.

"We're moving," she said when I came home from school and stared at her, where she sat in the living room, surrounded by stuff.

"Why?" I thought it was just a matter of paying the rent we owed. Dad would do it. He always bailed us out.

"Time for a change."

Turned out, she finally got a teaching position at one of the elementary schools and my father was helping her buy a house. I never saw Rob Calloway again.

"I remember you back then," Oliver said. "At school."

I couldn't look at him and we were quiet for the rest of the assembly. Later, on the way home in his car, he told me.

18.

Y ou used to wear this round, straw hat," Oliver said as he drove. We were nearly home from school. "Like a deep bowl on your head. You braided your hair. Wore those pants that were too long and frayed at the hem. We all thought you were some kind of spy."

"What are you talking about?" I asked him.

He pulled his car to the curb in front of my dad's house. "You. In junior high."

"You thought I was a spy?"

"Not really. But we thought you were pretty cool."

"I think the word you mean is weird. A freak."

He shook his head, looking past me out the window to the house. "Nobody ever thought you were weird. We always thought you were, I don't know, independent. You didn't need anybody. You did your own thing. I get it now, I think."

"What do you mean?" I had my hand on the door latch, wanting to leave.

"You'd been through a lot more than any of us had by that time. It showed. We just misinterpreted."

"Benny gave me the hat," I said. I tried to think what happened to it. It was probably buried under mounds of clothing and trash—taken out and burned after the coroner removed my mother's body from the hoard. At least, that's what I imagined had happened to all of our stuff. Dad and Jennie didn't let me go through it, anyway. They told me I was starting over fresh. Everything new. I think my dad believed that would erase all the bad that had happened since Will died. "See?" he seemed to say. Everything can be made right again. All you have to do is throw out the trash.

Before my mother and I moved from the apartment, I found Benny in the woods behind the convenience store, late one afternoon. He'd rigged himself up a little camp with tarps strung on trees and shrubs, worn lawn chairs and a wood crate for a table. There was evidence of a fire, but the spot was cold and damp. He'd been lying on a filthy quilt when I came upon him and he sat up, startled at first.

"The birthday girl," he said. "Lenore."

I sat on one of his chairs and looked around. The place smelled of trash and pot and I was surprised at how familiar the odor was—not much unlike home.

"I'm moving away. I won't be able to come by again. I didn't want you to think I didn't want to visit you."

He smiled and I noticed then that he had a few teeth missing. He scratched at his beard like he had fleas. Each of his fingernails was embedded with dirt; his hands were stained with mud and blood and God only knew what else.

"Far?"

"Across town."

"Well, then, we might see each other again. When I get back on my feet, get a job, you know?"

"Would you shave off your beard?"

He started pulling at it. "It's grown awfully long, hasn't it?"

"You should cut it off. You'll have a better chance at getting a job. And maybe take a shower."

"You're right. It's true enough."

"Where can you do that?"

"There really ain't nowhere to do that."

"You could do it at my apartment. Until I move, I mean."

He looked at me thoughtfully, almost like he didn't believe I'd said it. I stood and told him to come with me and we walked along the road to the apartment building. He was nervous—kept looking behind us, all around, like he thought someone might catch him doing something wrong. He'd brought along a change of clothes, the only other pants and shirt he had, he told me. I let him into our apartment and led him to the bathroom. I gave him a toothbrush from the cabinet and showed him where my razors were, but he said he'd just trim it with some scissors.

"It'll just have to grow out again." He caught the look on my face. "It itches something awful when it's growing out. A trim will be enough. You sure this is okay?"

"Course it is."

"When do you expect your mom will be home?"

"Take your time," I told him.

It was about an hour before he came out—shiny and damp. The bathroom let out steam into our little hallway. His old clothes hung over the shower curtain rod, dripping. He'd trimmed his beard close; it was a little bit ragged, but nicer than the scraggly mess he'd gone in with.

"I feel new," he said.

I could see then, that he was a young man. Though his eyes were lined and dark, like a man who'd live too many lives, the curve of his chin and cheeks was soft, untested. I got him some iced tea and we sat on the sofa.

"I haven't felt air conditioning in a long time," he said.

"Do you want to watch television?"

"No. The air conditioning is enough to miss later."

We sat silent for several moments and I turned to find him with his eyes closed, his head leaned back onto the sofa

"What happened to you?" I asked him.

His head popped up and he looked at me, surprised. He looked around our living room for a bit and then said, "I don't know. I was in Texas, living with my mom. I left—went looking for my dad. She always told me he was in Key West."

"Are you on your way down there?"

He shook his head. "I been there. I been all over the Keys. Nobody's heard of him."

"She lied?"

He looked at me, concern tugging his brows. "I guess so. Guess I should have told her I was leaving. Maybe she'd have confessed it."

"Do you want to call her? You can use our phone."

"I tried calling her. Collect. On the pay phones."

"She won't take your call?"

"She's not there."

"You can try again."

"No; I mean, she's gone. Somebody else has that number. You know what I think sometimes? Sometimes, when I've been walking for a long time and I'm tired and my eyes start blurring, I think I'm insane. I think I made it all up in my head. I think the woman I thought was my mother in Texas is just in my own imagination. And the father I'm looking for, too. Delusions."

I felt heavy when he said that—pulled into the couch like a boulder. "I know. Sometimes I think I'm making my life up, too."

"Maybe what we're making up is better than what's real."

"Maybe."

The front door opened and my mother came in carrying a brown grocery bag against her right hip and three plastic department store bags in her left hand. She set her bags on the little table in the dining area and looked at me and Benny before taking her grocery bag into the kitchen where she started putting her purchases away, cabinet doors opening and slamming shut.

"I should go," Benny said.

"Why?"

He didn't answer. We listened as my mother put all the groceries away. She came into the dining room and grabbed her plastic bags. She turned to us and nodded before leaving; we heard her bedroom door shut.

"Well," Benny said, "she's real enough."

I chuckled. "She's there," I told him. "But she's not real."

He laughed at that and grabbed the remote off the end table beside him. We watched Oprah and then he took his damp clothes from the bathroom and we walked together back to the main road.

"I'll come visit," I told him as we neared the convenience store.

"Now, Miss Lenore," he said, "how are you going to do that?"

At his spot in the woods, he hung his clothes on the scrawny branches of a scrub oak.

"I will," I said. "I promise."

He reached into one of his bags and pulled out the funny little hat. "Here." He handed it to me. "I found this on the road. It don't work on me. You take it."

I put in on my head and smiled for him. "How do I look?"

"Just like that," he said. "That's the way I'll remember you."

"But we'll see each other again. Like you said."

He nodded and tried to smile. "Sure we will. That's the truth."

I stood there, thinking I ought to hug him. But he didn't make a move. So I left him behind the store. A few days later, Mom and I moved into the little neighborhood near her school. She stopped having parties—became a responsible adult, as she liked to say. Everything on the outside was right; it appeared even...balanced—real. But the house wasn't full enough for her. The extra bedroom started out as a memorial to Will, but over time boxes and piles of clothes, newspapers, and junk took it over. She was building walls, I realized. Around herself. Keeping me out.

19.

Hannah and I figured we could get to Tampa and back without Mel knowing about it. I was worried. I mean, Hannah was barely seventeen. Taking her to Tampa was like kidnapping. I'd never been in trouble with the law before—not overtly. But barring any unforeseen events, Mel wouldn't have to know about it at all. And if she did find out, it would be over and done. What could she do about it then? Nothing, I figured. The girl came over as soon as Mel was off to work and hurried me out of the house after she fed the cats.

"Do we have to sit in the hot car the way you like?" she said.

"I guess not." We got in and instead of letting myself feel the heat, I turned the key right away and blasted her with AC. "You got snacks?"

"Yep," she said "Even found those orange crackers you wanted." She held up two packages of Lance crackers. "Mel didn't even ask about them. Did you put Coke in the cooler?"

"Just like you asked for."

I was surprised at how happy we both were. Myself, I hadn't felt giddy in an age. In fact, I tried not to think too hard on it. Remembering happiness would only lead to sadness. And Hannah was smiling, like a well-adjusted sort of teen. Not the kind I was used to dealing with on Sycamore Street. And certainly not the way I'd expect seeing as she was about to meet her mother. That started me worrying, and I let the joy seep out of me. She had her hopes up, I thought.

"Did you find the directions?" she asked.

I had told her I could look up the address she'd given me on the computer. "Better than that. I found this." I held up a box I'd dug out of the pile of shipping boxes in the front room.

"What's that? Holy cow, a GPS." She grabbed it from me as I backed out of the driveway.

"Plug the thing in and get it working."

After she'd played with it and it started talking to us, telling us how to find I95, like we didn't know, we settled down and I turned on the radio. "Tune it to whatever station you like," I told her.

"What do *you* like?"

"I grew up on disco and hard rock."

She rolled her eyes, but she was smiling. She found a local rock station and started singing along. Once we were near the 528 exit, I asked her, "Why wouldn't Mel let you get your license?"

She sighed. "I got my learner's permit."

I waited for her to go on, trying not to prod too much.

"Mel told me if I kept out of trouble for a year, I could get it when I turn eighteen. She said seventeen's too young, anyway. God, she's so oppressive."

"It's her job to oppress you. It's what mother's do."

She glared at me and then turned to look out the window.

"When are you eighteen?" I said, trying to redirect us. I didn't want the girl mad at me for the entire drive to Tampa.

"In October. But I got Ds in algebra and P.E. last year."

"I get you. I hated P.E., too."

"I cut that class. A lot. Could be worse. I know a girl who failed it. She has to take it in summer school. Can you imagine? Running around the track in the summer?"

"The death toll will be high."

At that, she let out a loud laugh. The air conditioner seemed to have finally cooled the car and everything lightened up.

"So, your license..."

"She said if I behave I can get it before Christmas. If I *behave*. Like I'm a three-year-old. 'Course, then she caught me out past curfew with Nicky. I don't even dare ask about it, now. She'll probably make me wait until I graduate. I don't care. I don't have a car to drive anyway, so what good is a license?"

"But you could drive Mel's on the weekends."

"Yeah." She sighed.

"And you don't have a phone?"

"Don't even get me started on that. I swear Mel lives in the Sixties or something. She doesn't understand that everybody has a phone and a computer these days. She has a laptop but she only lets me use it for school stuff. I feel so backward."

"You could have looked your mom up, if you had a phone or a computer."

"You think Mel's keeping them from me on purpose?" There was the edge of a smile at her lips.

"I doubt it. You could always use your friends' computers."

"I don't really know any kids like that."

She went on talking and I let her. The thing is, I did look up her mother's address on my computer. After I managed to dig it out from under a pile of shoes. I wanted to tell her what I found, but I couldn't. I told myself that she wouldn't believe me anyway; she'd insist on seeing for herself. And she'd be right. This was a lesson she was going to have to work through by herself or it wouldn't sink in. I think about it now, looking back on it, and I wonder if I'd taken her to Tampa if I'd known the truth.

20.

A few days after we moved into the little house, my mom drove me to a place on the western edge of town, out near the trash complex. She pulled up to a gate, rolled her window down, and punched some numbers into a box on a post. The gate swung open and she drove through rows of garages built into long strips of building. She stopped and told me to get out. With keys, she unlocked two garage doors and then lifted them up—they rolled into the ceilings. And inside, stuffed into the spaces, was junk. Junk I remembered vaguely—stuff that hadn't made it to Grandma's or our apartment.

"I kept it all," she said with a smile. "I knew we'd have a house one day."

Of course, the stuff she'd taken from Will's room wasn't there. That had been stolen from our car that night at Grandma's. But there was plenty of other stuff, including my bicycles—that first one she bought me after Will died and every one she bought each year after that. We made a dozen trips back and forth, loading up the car and dumping everything in the house—anywhere, she said. It didn't matter. So long as we could find it when we needed it. That was her philosophy. At some point, she turned her back on that sort of thing. I suppose I did too. When it gets to the point that you can't really find anything at all—when your piles of possessions are walls of a maze instead of anything remotely useful, you decide that it's only important that you remember it. When you bought it, from where, what it looked like, what it felt like in your hands, how much you paid for it. That was enough—memory was enough. It had to be.

Our house was little, but it had a third bedroom. I feared that she would want to recreate Will's room in it—feared that she was still stuck in that space where Will lived—but she didn't. She talked and talked about that room and what we could do with it. A sitting room, where we could watch television or read. An office, with a desk and typewriter. A sewing room. That was her favorite choice. The sewing machine and ironing board were already in there and we kept from putting anything else in there, at first. But as the loads came from the storage units, she weakened.

"Oh, that," she said about the box of crafting books. "Those can go in the sewing room. They're related, right?" And the boxes and bags of old clothes could be put in there. They could be mended, altered, or better yet, cut up and used for new sewing projects. "Just think of the things we could make," she said, not to me but to herself. By the end of the sixth trip we were loading the spare room up with boxes without bothering to look inside them. "We can organize later." I knew that wasn't going to happen. I wonder if she did.

The back porch, outside a sliding glass door, was framed with aluminum; bits of green screening, ripped and torn, fluttered in the wind at all the corners. The door was missing, but it wasn't needed. A worn wooden fence protected us from the neighbors and a greenish trunked orange tree struggled in the back right corner of the yard.

"We need a swing," she said.

I told her I wasn't six anymore.

"A grownup swing. One that seats two. Right there," she pointed toward the tree.

"For us?"

"And a garden of azaleas and roses and forget-me-nots. I love forget-me-nots."

"Do you even know what they look like?"

"Who cares?" she said.

I didn't understand how she could look out on the back yard, tufts of grass that would never grow to fill in the dirt spots, and see possibilities, when she had to know that it would end up filled with stuff. Not even lawn care stuff. I could see it all: bags and boxes and plastic bins with lids. Old tires and car parts and the first few major appliances that stopped working. I'm not sure where the vision came from or why I saw it, but I did. I'd given up or given in. I wanted the empty space filled and I didn't want to pretend otherwise.

On that first Saturday at the new house, I slipped out early, before my mother was awake and rode my bike across town. I wore cut-offs I'd made from some blue jeans and my legs felt weird out in the open—bare and exposed. The wind whipped my hair into my face no matter how much I tried to keep it tucked behind my ears. I squinted against the bright, Florida sun and sweat wet my clothes, despite the wind. But I didn't care. I wanted to see Benny again. I rode down Barna to Knox McRae and west to Park Avenue. It was farther than I thought it would be and when I finally came to the convenience store, I was parched and could feel the heat in my cheeks. I walked my bike around to the back of the store and into the wooded lot where I found Benny's little patch—empty. His chairs were there, the cooler sat open on its side with ants crawling inside it. I spied his sleeping bag rolled up and stashed in the bushes. I took a seat—the chair creaked loudly in the quiet of the trees—to wait. As I sat, my breathing evened out and the perspiration on my face dried up. I combed through my hair with my fingers and played with it, rolling it up in buns and braiding it, only to let it swing free. Every tick of a branch or thump on the ground startled me, but Benny didn't show up. I could feel tears battling to get through and a cry welling up in my throat.

It wasn't until I got home, flushed from the sun and heat, walked in and found my mother sitting in the front room digging through a box, tossing wadded up bits of newspaper over her shoulder that I realized why I'd cried all the way home. She turned to look at me, nodded, and went back to her box.

Benny looked me in the eyes. He acted as if I was a person. A part of me, I think, knew that there would come a time when it would be too late to save me.

21.

I remembered that day when I drove Hannah across the state to Tampa—remembered that hollow feeling I had in my gut as I rode my bike across town to find Benny. Somehow, I knew I wouldn't see him. Because if I had, I planned on staying with him, never going back home. I think we all know how our lives are going to turn out; we just look away from it if it's not appealing. We see what's going on around us. We see our places in the world and in the hearts of our parents and we work it out from there. I saw the future and I wanted out of it. Benny was the first person, since Will died, who'd looked me straight in the face and smiled. He was my savior. But he was already lost to me.

And I felt that way for Hannah, as we made our way to her mother's house. The girl had to know already, the truth that she would be coming home again with me. Her mother wouldn't take her in. If her mother wanted her, she'd have got her. But just as that yearning to be somebody special drove me on my bike, Hannah's need to be loved by her mother drove her to the other coast—no matter what the truth of it was. No matter what she told me later. I couldn't tell if I was helping or hurting by my part in it.

She chatted for the first hour and after that, we were quiet. As we hit the city, about another hour after that, she started playing with her hands in her lap. She glanced up at the GPS monitor often, checking to see if our arrival time had changed. It hadn't. I left the interstate and drove west on a big highway, then took a right into suburbs. Down a long and winding road, dotted with large houses. Her hands were clasped, squeezing. At the time, I thought it was because she didn't expect this—a good neighborhood with fancy mailboxes shaped like pelicans and manatees. I guess the reality was that she was nervous. When I turned into the subdivision, with its huge signs on either side of the road, decorated with flowering allamanda, she flattened her hands against her thighs and rubbed the sweat off on her jeans. Then she left them there, grasping her legs. I drove up the curving driveway to her mother's fancy house and parked just before it rounded the turn to the front door. I pulled the key out of the ignition.

Hannah sat still for a moment while the cool air seeped out of the windows and the heat began to pour in. "Are you coming with me?" she said.

I sighed. "No. You have to do this yourself."

She nodded, slightly. Of course, now I know that she didn't want me too close. She didn't want me to know the truth. I suppose I can forgive her for that.

"Don't be afraid," I said. "This is stuff you have to know. One way or the other."

She nodded again, fainter, barely. I thought she was in shock—her mother was supposed to be a drug addict, unable to care for her own child. But there she was, living the grand life. I thought Hannah was scared, worried, feeling the brunt of being shunned all over again. Looking back on it all, I wonder what she was really thinking.

"You heard of that cat, right?" I said.

Finally life returned to her eyes and face; she looked at me, questioning.

"Schrodinger's cat."

"Huh?" she said.

"Schrodinger was a scientist. He proposed a thought experiment. Something to do with quantum mechanics; I can't remember the specifics. Anyway, imagine a cat in a box and when something is triggered, a poison will be released, killing the cat. But you don't know when that will happen, or if it has happened. So, for you, the cat is neither alive, nor dead, until you open the box and look at it."

"So?"

"So you can't live like that. And frankly, neither can the cat. You have to open the box and find out. Is she the woman who was forced to give you up? Or did Mel save you from a monster? Or some other scenario that you can't possibly know until you walk up there and knock."

"What if I don't want to know?"

"Hannah," I glared at her. "You already know. All that's left is the knocking." I had no idea at the time how right I was.

"If I already know," she said, "what does the cat have to do with anything?"

She had me stumped there, almost; and I was never one to admit defeat quickly. "The cat story just means you have to go out there and be sure."

You had to give the girl some credit, when you put it all together. She knew how to get what she wanted. She stared at the front door and I followed her gaze. The curtains in the front window shuddered. The woman knew we were there. I turned back to her. Her lips were pursed and her brow creased. Anger was good, I thought. Maybe she was going to be all right, after all. She pulled the car door open and stepped out. I watched her back as she walked up the driveway—watched as she went from upright and determined to slouched and fearful. But damn it if the girl didn't keep walking, right up to the front porch, right up to the door, where she reached out, hesitated, and pushed the doorbell.

We both waited. I imagined the shrew on the other side of the door, her breath catching in her throat, wondering what in the hell she was going to do.

"Come on, bitch," I whispered. "Open the door."

She did...a sliver. I couldn't see her face. Then a little more. Then the bitch slid herself out onto the porch and closed the door behind her so fast it was as if she'd practiced this whole scene. She was bleached blond, hair to her shoulders, wearing a white sun dress and sandals. I couldn't see the nails from where I sat, but I knew they were manicured and dainty. I could see, however, the diamonds glittering off her wrist. And when she turned to glance at the car, I saw her rigid smile. She put a hand on Hannah's shoulder and led her off the porch, back onto the driveway, toward the car.

"What the hell?" I said.

They talked. Hannah stood with her hands clasped in front of her. Her mother was angry. Hannah grabbed her own elbows. Her mother was suddenly nervous. Finally, Hannah's hands were up on her shoulders, her arms across her chest, protecting herself. Her mother rolled her eyes, flippant, and her head jerked back to the house. Suddenly, the woman was angry again. I watched as Hannah took a slight step back from her. Before I knew what had happened, Hannah's mother had turned and left her standing alone on the driveway. I thought maybe the woman had gone in to get her something. A memento. The stuffed bear she had as a baby. Her blanket. Maybe the woman had covered her baby shoes in copper. But she didn't come back and when Hannah turned to the car and started walking, I saw everything in her shudder and shift. She was triumphant at first—filled with the anger she ought to have, after such an altercation. But the closer she got to the car, the more it ran from her. Furious to devastated in a matter of five seconds.

I was pissed off. That bitch talked to her daughter for about three minutes and then told her to leave. Hannah was crying, still holding on to herself. It was only as I turned my gaze back to the house, while she climbed into the car, and saw everything blurred that I realized I was crying too.

22.

I don't remember high school graduation. I don't remember telling Oliver to go out with his friends and leave me alone that night. I don't remember getting up out of bed at two a.m. and going into the bathroom. I do, however, remember the razor blade against my wrists—exquisite—and the hot water of the bathtub. I used a fresh replacement blade for a box cutter that I'd found out in the garage, on my dad's workbench. Everything was so neat and tidy at his house—everything had its place, except me. So it was odd that I'd come home a few weeks before to find the box cutter lying on the table with the cheap cardboard container of blades, open, next to it. It shouldn't have been left out like that. It must have been meant for me. I took one. I probably knew then what I planned to do; but I hid it from myself.

I remember screaming, but Jennie told me there wasn't any of that. She said she and Dad were stunned—too horrified to say a word. She'd heard the bath running and knocked. Then pounded on the door calling my name. My father broke the door, rushed at it. Very heroic. He dragged me out of the tub and wrapped strips of a t-shirt around my wrists while Jennie called for the ambulance. I've wondered about it for so many years—who was screaming? I used to think I was replaying that day at the beach and it was my mother, screaming for Will. But as soon as Dr. Melvin said the word cancer, I heard the screaming again. It's just me. Inside my head.

I didn't see Oliver for a long time after that. Jennie and Dad told me he came to the house nearly every day to ask about me, but they wouldn't allow him at the hospital.

"You need to concentrate on yourself right now," Jennie said to me. As if that meant anything at all.

I could see the question on their faces, the one they were too afraid to ask. Why? Or maybe they didn't ask because they knew already. They saw my bedroom—saw the collection of empty water bottles I'd strung together with embroidery thread and a thick needle. They saw the bookshelves crowded with magazines and school work I couldn't throw away. All those bits of trash from the bathroom that Jennie insisted I clean up were kept in plastic grocery bags in one corner: used Q-tips, nearly empty toothpaste tubes, the paper toilet tissue wrappers and the empty rolls. It's funny how that worked out. My mother was gone. Her stuff was gone. Her wallet, too. I hadn't the means to collect anything worthwhile, so I built my defense with trash.

It was only a week before Oliver was to pack up and move to Atlanta for school. One night, he came and got me from my dad's and walked me across and down the street to his house. He spread a sheet on the back lawn. The grass was lush and cool to the touch, even in summer. We lay down on our backs, felt the grass crinkle against us, and looked at the stars. He took my hand and our fingers laced together. I closed my eyes.

"I do understand," he said.

I was going to tell him that was impossible. But it would only lead to more questions. I'd realized when I took the blade off Dad's work bench, I suppose, that there was no way I could tell Oliver the truth. I could feel myself burying it, storing it away. I think that's why I got into the tub. I didn't want to live with it like that—way down deep where it could fester and ruin me, eat at me year after year. God only knew what it would turn me into.

"You've been working up to it," he said. "Trying to tell me something really bad. You're afraid I'll dump you when I find out...whatever it is. But I won't."

I still didn't respond. No matter how long he waited. I had nothing to say.

"I love you," he said.

It must have been shock that made me blurt out, "She forced me to do it."

"What?"

"The abortion. My mother forced me."

Tommy lived next door with his father who worked nights and slept all day. He never paid me any attention until I was sixteen. Suddenly he was always outside when I came home from school and on the weekends. He offered to do odd jobs for my mother. He laid sod and mowed it every week once it had taken root. He dragged everything out of the garage, organized it, swept the space and sprayed it down with insecticide, and then put everything back in. And he talked to me the whole time. He was trying to get a band together to tour the whole United States, maybe even Europe. He wore tight pants and loose tank tops. His hair hung down his back like black moss on a tree and he kept it out of his face with a handkerchief tied into a knot on his forehead. He was beautiful. Everything was dark about him but his blue eyes—animal, earthy. I invited him inside for some iced tea. He stood outside the tiny kitchen, near the table, looking around at the stacks of boxes and bags of trash.

"Still moving in?"

"No." I was trembling when I handed him the glass and he noticed. He mistook my fear for anticipation, but I didn't mind.

I'd spent the last two years doing my best to hide from men. I kept myself wrapped up in overlong corduroys and unflattering t-shirts. But that day, I stood in the little dining room of my mother's house in a blush pink bikini eying Tommy Alvarez like a wolf. He sipped the tea, watching me.

"How old are you, now?" he asked.

"Sixteen."

"I'm too old for you, you know."

I nodded.

He set the glass on the table, reached out, and pulled me to him, kissing me hard. His lips were ice cold and wet, slippery. It happened so fast—right there on the floor in the dining room, in that little space carved out of my mother's hoard—that I didn't have time to be afraid.

It was a few months later that I started vomiting. My mother glared at me every morning. I knew what was happening and I found myself able to smile, hum, dance a little bit through the house. She didn't say anything. Not to me. It was when I hadn't seen Tommy for about a week that I went next door and spoke to Mr. Alvarez.

"He's gone down to Miami," he told me. "Can't risk jail."

"Jail?"

"She said it was rape, your mother did."

And then she started working on me. I couldn't raise a child on my own and she wouldn't help me. If I didn't go to the women's clinic on Saturday, she'd put me out of the house. My father and Jennie would never take me in. She laughed at the thought of it. I said nothing to her and it enraged her. She threw a bag of shoes at me, called me a whore, told me the appointment was made. It was after the procedure, when I was curled up in bed in the dark of the evening, that she told me the truth.

"I can't let you do it," she said. "Not until I'm gone."

"Why?"

She didn't answer me, but I knew—it was Will. It was always him. She was terrified of looking into the eyes of her grandchild, and seeing her son.

Oliver whispered, "I'm sorry."

"It wasn't so much that I loved Tommy," I said. "But I wanted that baby."

It was wrong of me, really. Because I wanted—needed—to be loved. Looking back on it, I realize that someone like me, someone who grew up without it, was hardly the right person to give love. In the end, perhaps, it all worked out for the best. But at the time, a hatred simmered inside me, fueled by resentment and pain; it grew more ragged and sharp with every drink my mother took, with every hurtful word she said, and with every wistful look at her hands thinking of Will. I seethed with it for almost two years, until my mother suffocated beneath her hoard and I thought I'd been set free.

23.

Hannah climbed into the car and slammed the door shut. I reached for the ignition, but she stopped me. "Not yet," she said.

I didn't question it, not out loud. If she thought the bitch was going to change her mind and come back out, she was going to be disappointed. I saw nothing in the woman's face but fear and shame and, yes, contempt.

"You want to roll down a window?" I asked her. "I don't mind."

"No."

I could see the sweat beading up on her temples.

"I get it now," she said. "The heat. Why you like it. It feels...like hell. Like punishment. Like what I deserve."

"What?"

"The heat."

"That ain't what it's about at all. Not for you. What did you do to deserve the heat?"

She shook her head.

"No, Hannah. Look at me." She did. She was sucking the hot air into her lungs through her nose like it was a battle. I rolled down my window, but it wasn't enough. I turned the ignition and blasted the air conditioner at us, put the car in gear and left the house, waiting for it to cool. It didn't take long. As hot as it was, we hadn't been there long enough—the woman had disowned her child in just a few minutes. "You don't need the heat to remind you of what you've done," I told her. "The heat isn't a punishment."

"Then why do you like it so much?" I could hear, in her voice, the tremors of rage and abandonment. She was going to let loose at any second and I'd have to pull over, grab her and hold her close. I hadn't touched another human being like that since Oliver, since that day I made him leave me. I wasn't sure I'd be able to endure it, and even if I could, for how long? This girl needed her grandmother. I let my foot sink a bit harder onto the gas pedal.

"I don't know," I said. "I think it's like my house, the heat. It surrounds me, better than all my stuff, because it even gets into my throat, my lungs. It's not suffocating; that's not what I'm trying to do. It's...well, it's like a hug."

We were silent for a while. I was still thinking about him. I could see him standing on the little front porch of my apartment. He'd driven all the way from Georgia, nonstop, he said, to see me. Why wouldn't I answer the phone? Why wouldn't I write back? What was happening? I shut the door behind me and stepped toward him, letting him pull me into his arms. It was late September, only a few weeks since he'd gone off to school in the first place. I thought I could just let it end that way—let him leave and start up a new life. He'd forget me in time. He'd have so much to do at college, and so many other girls to consider. But there he stood that Saturday afternoon, his face red and wet with sweat, his body heat seeping into my chest. I pulled away and stepped back.

"It's done, Oliver. You know it's done."

"What's done?"

"Us. We need to let it be finished."

He shook his head and reached for me, but I stopped

him.

"What are you saying?" His voice was quiet, almost a whisper—as if he didn't want to ask. He didn't want the answer. "We've been over this. I'll be home at Christmas and spring break and all summer. We can do this."

"You've talked about it. I never said it would work."

"But it *will* work. It *can* work."

"No."

The confusion on his face hardened into anger. "Why not? If you don't love me anymore, say so."

"I don't love you, Oliver."

"That's a lie."

"It doesn't matter." I heard the neighbor's window slide up. Fine; let her listen. "It's over. I need you to go now. I need you to find your life without me."

"But why? Is this about all your stories? You know I don't care about any of that. If I cared, I wouldn't still be here."

"There's more," I said. "I didn't tell you everything."

"Then tell me."

"No." We were at a stalemate. I knew it; but he didn't seem to understand.

"Just tell me the rest of it and we can get past it."

"I'm done, Oliver. It's over."

"I can't accept that."

I was angry now. "You don't have a choice."

"You can't do this, Lenore."

"I can. I'm doing it."

"But why?"

"Please leave." I turned to pull open the door. He reached out to grab my arm, but let it go when I glared back at him.

"Please," he said. "Tell me why. I deserve a reason."

I stood there, angry, sweating, trembling. Just tell him, I was thinking. Just say it. Tell him the truth. He does deserve to know why. Say it. But I couldn't. I turned the knob, pulled the door open, and slipped inside my apartment.

"Lenore, wait," he said as I shut the door.

I know he heard me turn the dead bolt.

He knocked. "Lenore," he said. "Tell me." He knocked again. "I'm not leaving until you give me a reason." He pounded his fists on the door. "Lenore!" I could feel his body leaning against mine, only the door between us. "Please," he begged. "You're killing me, Lenore. You're killing me."

I started to cry then. I pushed myself off the door and ran into my bedroom where he wouldn't hear me.

"Talk to me," Hannah said, pulling me back. I'd already got onto the Interstate without realizing it. "I'm going to break if you don't talk."

"I could play the radio." My voice cracked a bit and I realized I was still upset about Oliver, even after all these years.

"I'd rather hear you talk."

"What do you want me to talk about?"

"What's in the envelope?"

"What?"

"The one you wanted me to find. What's in it? Tell me the story. I won't even be listening really, if it's a secret. I just need to hear your voice."

"Why?"

"I just...never mind."

"No, no. I'll talk. I'll tell you."

I thought about how much to tell. We had two hours ahead of us. I hadn't talked for two hours straight in my entire life. But I was sure I understood what Hannah was after—the voice. "I should start with Oliver," I said. "Even though he's not the beginning. Oliver is...or should have been, the end, and so I think it's proper to start with him."

She let her head fall back onto the headrest and closed

her eyes.

When we arrived back at the house, Mel was standing outside, her arms crossed at her chest, waiting for us. Of all the days to pop home for lunch and worry when she couldn't find Hannah. The air conditioning on the ride home wasn't enough to keep me cool. The pain of talking, telling Hannah most of the things I didn't really want to remember, thrust a twisted dull knife in my chest. I choked on each breath I took as I left the car and watched Hannah fall into her grandmother's embrace. All the anger washed out of Mel in an instant. When she lifted her eyes over Hannah's head to look at me, I knew something was wrong. I could feel the life leaving me.

This couldn't be it, I thought; could it? Cancer doesn't drop you with a single hack of the axe, like, say, jumping from the roof of a building would. No, I realized, as I felt my knees buckle and everything around me went dark. This is just the heat, claiming me.

Part Two
Hannah

24.

I fainted once, last April. I was sitting in psychology class. It was near end of term and Mrs. Portgill was playing around with us. She told us to close our eyes and take ourselves back through time, to find our earliest memory. Find that first place you remember, she told us. That first house, first room. It might only be a tiny glimpse but hold on to it. Then we opened our eyes and she clapped her hands. "Okay, let's share." She started around the room, that much I remember, but the rest is dark and confused. Stacy Klemp, who sat next to me, told me I tried to stand up and fell. She thought I'd got my legs twisted up in the chair legs. Mrs. Portgill, she said, made everybody stop laughing, and came to me. "Hannah," she called. "Hannah."

Apparently I woke up. She had the dean come to the classroom and walk me to the clinic. He asked me a lot of stupid questions. Did I eat breakfast? When was the last time I ate anything? Was I taking any kind of medication? Then at the clinic, the nurse asked me the same questions again. They made me lie down and the nurse was shining a light in my eyes. She felt my head. I could feel the lump beneath her fingers. Mel had to come to the school and take me home. I had to go to the doctor to see if I had a concussion.

At dinner time that night, Mel came to my bedroom with a plate on a tray and asked me if I felt like eating. I didn't. She sat on the edge of the bed and patted my leg. I stared down at the plate of food. It looked like hospital food. Clean and tasteless. A half of chicken breast baked. Some cooked carrots. Peas. Mel could do better than that, I thought.

"It was fainting," she said. "It happens sometimes. Did you eat breakfast?"

I rolled my eyes. We were both quiet for a moment while I studied the piece of wheat bread on the plate. Where was the butter?

"What happened to my dad?" I asked her.

She moved her hand from my leg. "What do you mean?"

"After we left him. Where did he go? Why didn't I ever see him again?"

"After you left him?"

"When we moved in with you, in that apartment."

She shook her head and eyed me, confused.

"What?" I said.

"You never lived with your father."

I looked up at her then. I can't describe it—the sudden realization that I'd been taut, ready to break, and hadn't noticed until I could finally breathe freely. "Trevor wasn't my dad?"

"No."

And then I started crying—sobbing really. That sick sort of crying you see people do on the cop shows when they find out someone they love has been murdered. Mel took the tray off my lap and sat closer, pulling me to her chest.

"What is it?" she kept saying. "What is it?"

It took me a while, and a bunch of tissues, to calm down. And when I did, I told her about the exercise we did in Psychology class. I told her that I remembered Trevor and the old apartment we lived in.

Trevor was wiry and pale and he used to like to lie back on the sofa with his bony feet, wide apart, on the coffee table. The TV would be on but he'd be looking up at the ceiling, blowing cigarette smoke, watching it float around. He always had a hand stuck in his pants. The first few times he took my hand—I was three, I think, almost four—and shoved it down into his underwear against his skin, I didn't understand. I didn't like it, and I knew somehow it was wrong, but I didn't know what was happening. The last time he did it, he wouldn't let my hand go. He made me rub him until he gasped and my mom came in and found us. She slapped me off the sofa and then fell on top of Trevor screaming.

Mel had hold of my shoulders, squeezing. Her eyes were wide open, her lips pulled tight together. "I didn't know that."

"I remember after we moved to your apartment," I said. "You had a sofa, too. I never sat on it, but I don't think you or Mom noticed." She shook her head. "Some women came over to visit, not too long after we moved in, and one of them picked me up, kissed my cheek, and carried me over to the sofa and sat down."

Mel gasped. "You screamed. You threw a fit. You kicked that woman, and anyone else that tried to hold you. I didn't know."

"It's okay. I don't think I knew, either."

"You were so little."

"Mom never told you?"

"No. I'm sorry." She sat up straight and sighed.

"I guess I forgot, over time."

"And you thought Trevor was your father. You did call him Daddy; I remember. But you stopped that."

"If he wasn't my father, who was?"

Mel got up and slipped off her shoes. She went to the

other side of the bed, threw the covers back and crawled in, scooting over next to me. She put her arm around me. "Here," she said. "You're going to need a cuddle."

I let it be. I used to let Mel cuddle me all the time, before the age of twelve. If I scraped a knee, or got into trouble, everything could be made better with a good long moment in her arms with my head tucked under her chin.

"It's like this," she said. "And what I'm going to tell you is something Casey didn't want you to know...ever. But I knew the time would come. And I know it should have come long before now. But I'd look at you and imagine your reaction and what it would mean and I never could manage to bring myself to find the right moment. Now's as good a time as ever."

I waited, thinking the worst—he was dead. My mother murdered him. He killed himself. Something awful.

But instead, Mel said, "Your mother didn't even know your dad."

25.

My mom would tell you I was lying before I could talk. And I don't know, I guess it's true enough. There were plenty good reasons to lie. If you're going to get hit either way, you might as well at least try a better story. And it worked a few times. I remember hiding the things I stole in a corner of my closet in that first little apartment we lived in before we moved into Mel's.

I wonder now, why my mom never told Mel about Trevor and the sofa. Especially after the screaming incident. I mean, I didn't get the connection, either. But I was three—things are hard to piece together when you're all caught up in them. Now that I can see it better, though, who wouldn't put the two together? My mom ought to have understood it. "Oh, right," she'd tell Mel. "Trevor molested Hannah on the sofa so maybe we shouldn't try to make her sit there." Honestly, I don't think my mother was that...smart. I'd heard my Uncle Everett say she was smart a few times, because she married this rich guy and moved across state. That was smart to him. I always figured it was dumb—I mean, it was dumb that got her the gig. I've met the husband and let me tell you, he's not the type who wants a smart wife. Anyway, the point is, I'm a liar. I know I'm a liar.

And part of me doesn't care.

I hated Mel for a long time. And here again, you don't see things clearly when it's all going to hell around you. But I see it plain as day now. I wanted Mel to give me away, the same as my mother had done. I needed Mel to prove to me that I was as worthless as I'd decided I was. That's what people do—they set out to get the world to agree with how they see themselves. You've got your smart-asses running around telling everyone how great they are and if you don't kiss their smart ass, to hell with you. And then you've got the Hannahs who make sure everybody thinks they're liars and thieves and worthless and if you don't agree, if you don't turn your back on them, they'll hate you for it. And that was my problem with Mel. She was always giving. Always understanding. Firm, sure, but never screaming at me like my mom.

I did about everything I could think of—not consciously of course—to piss my grandmother off and make her throw me out on the street. And at the same time—get this—I was scared that one day she'd do just that. The human psyche is batshit crazy, isn't it? I stole everything I wanted to steal. Before we moved in with Mel, it was toys and candy. I stole from the stores we went into—mostly dollar stores—and I stole from other kids at the playground at our apartment complex. Mom found my stash one day, in the back corner of my closet. I know she found it because it was all taken out and spread across my bedroom carpet. I'll never know, I guess, if she left it there like that because she wanted me to know she knew about it, or if she was just too lazy to put it all back. Either way, when I came out of my room and into the kitchen, she turned to me and slapped me across the face. It was left to me to put the two together: my stash exposed, a slap in the face. But there was always doubt.

At Mel's, there was no playground. A lobby took up

142

most of the first floor of her apartment building and, behind that, a big room for having parties—Mel had one, once, and let me come in to meet her fancy friends before a babysitter took me upstairs. The rest of the space was made up of business offices. There was one place...a real estate office, I think, that had a bowl of hard candy on the front desk. I'd walk past, back and forth, waiting for the receptionist to go to the bathroom. Then I'd run in, grab handfuls of candy and dart into the elevator before she got back. She had to know it was me.

When my mother left, Mel told me she was stuck with me and we moved into a proper house. Okay, she didn't say that, exactly. She said, "It's me and you now, Hannah." And then I think she said some weird sort of motivational stuff about how we had to stick together. She told me my mother wasn't able to take care of me; but she'd do whatever she could. I knew the truth. And she knew I knew. My mother didn't want me. I knew it the first time Gary Minna came to pick her up and take her out. His suit was shiny. I'm not kidding. Shiny, like satin. He had this huge gold watch on his wrist, gold cuff links—I was five by then, mind you, and didn't know what they were—and thick gold chains hanging down his hairy chest beneath his unbuttoned fancy shirt. He smelled like perfume and his hair was slicked back. I thought he was the President. But he wasn't. He was just Gary Minna. The rich guy who wanted my mother, but not me.

After they got married, I got to go visit about once a month until my mother got pregnant. Then it was pretty much over. Gary made no secret of it. He'd say it right in front of me. "She can't be here once the baby is born. You can go to the other coast, if you want. But you won't be taking the baby." My mom didn't think about it long. She never came to visit. She called me on the phone a few times. Or, maybe Mel called her and I talked to her. She'd tell me how hard it was, raising a baby. She promised to come over to see me as soon as things settled down. They never did. Except for that one time when I was nine.

26

It was a big day—even though it was only me and Mel, everything was rushed and excited. Mom and Gary were coming over to see me. I got to stay out of school and Mel made me comb my hair and put on nice clothes. It had been almost three years by then, since I'd seen my mother and I was nervous. I thought she was coming to take me home with her and I was afraid if I didn't behave just right, Gary would change his mind and I'd be left again. I don't know where I got the idea—Mel certainly didn't tell me. But she made such a fuss. I'd been told that my half-brother and the baby weren't coming, so I knew something very important was happening. Something special. And even as I prayed it was all for me, I knew it couldn't be.

We were in our little house on Sycamore then and I don't like to think back on me standing at the front window watching for the car to come down the street. It's like...it's not me. It's a sweet kid, not the little lying thief I knew I was. I knew what I was, because I'd heard my mother say it. Mel once told me a story about my mother and how much she loved me—all the wonderful things she said about me.

"She thinks the world of you, sweetheart," Mel said. "She asks me, every time we talk, 'how's my little darling?'"

I knew she was lying. It's funny how one bad thing screws up any good thing that comes after. But it does. I know not everybody wants to believe that. They say crap like, you can undo a negative thought with just one good, positive thought. Well, that's bullshit. It doesn't matter how many times your mother smiles at you and tells you you're wonderful. Once she's called you a lying, thieving, little piss you know anything good she says has got some kind of hook to it. Usually the hook was, 'be nice to Gary.'

When they finally arrived that day, and came into the tiny front room, I could feel the tension among us all, like a fog, holding us still. My mom was wearing a blue suit, with a skirt hemmed below the knee. She looked so tidy and prim—I didn't really recognize her, but Mel was smiling at her, so I accepted it. She leaned down and kissed my cheek, then turned away, taking a seat on the sofa. Gary didn't even look at me, but sat beside her. I sat on the edge of the big easy chair watching the three of them talking. Gary did most of it. Mel asked him about Tampa, about the kids—my half brother and sister—about the trip over. I didn't pay much attention. My ears were buzzing. I watched her. Her hands folded neatly in her lap. She was trembling. I looked at her face—she was smiling but her forehead was pulled together.

When Mel got up to get them iced tea, I said, "Mommy's sick."

Gary put a protective hand over hers, but neither of them said a thing.

Of course, they didn't take me with them when they left. It all makes sense now.

"When she was fifteen," Mel told me, curled up on the bed with me that day last May. "Your mother went to a party with a friend. It was at a house in our neighborhood. This was before your grandfather died. Do you remember him?"

I shook my head against her chest.

146

"No, I suppose not. He died when you were barely a year old. Anyway, we lived over by the country club. It's not as fancy as it sounds." She was stalling and I was about to say something. "So, what happened was…your mom's friend met a boy there and she left with him. Your mom had to walk home alone. And she was…" Her voice wobbled a bit. "Someone attacked her." Before I could sit fully up to look at her, she'd said, "You mother was raped."

I climbed off the bed and stood looking at her like she was a crazy person. She started going on and on about how sorry she was to have kept the truth from me and then she launched in on my mother. What a sacrifice my mother made to keep me, to try to raise me. That might not be exactly how she said it, but that was pretty much what she meant, wasn't it? I was a stain. A reminder of something awful. How fortunate I was that she didn't abort me. And I just stood there. Finally, Mel came off the bed and over to me.

"Did I do the right thing in telling you?" she asked.

I wanted to laugh. She wanted reassurance? I think I nodded and she encouraged me to eat. She said we'd talk later. And we did. I learned that when I was nine and Gary and Mom came to see me, they were only there for the trial. They'd finally caught the guy and the women he raped all testified against him.

Once the school year finally ended, Mel came to me that first Saturday afternoon, standing at the door in my bedroom. "You're getting back to yourself," she said. "Are you feeling better? Any questions left?"

I told her no. I don't know why she thought I was better. The thing is, all my life I thought my mother left me for a man. But, it turns out, she left me…because of me. Before, my mom was the awful person. And now it was me.

I told this to Nicky that night. He said it was all bullshit. "But they're parents, so what do you expect?"

I look back at it now, and I don't understand it. I loved my mother and I knew she didn't want me. And I hated Mel for wanting me. What the hell was that all about? And I think I'd still be right there in all that, if it weren't for Mrs. Hawn. And seriously...think about it. I'd never have met Mrs. Hawn proper like, if it weren't for Nicky. Imagine that! Nicky. Doing something right for a change.

27.

I'd met Nicky in the park across the way about a year ago. I guess that's not entirely true. He and I both grew up, pretty much, in that neighborhood with Mel.

I was what they called "troubled." I got suspended a lot. Even in third grade. I was that little girl putting gum in other girls' hair, stomping on bare toes with my heel, hitting and shoving on the playground. I was not a bully. Let's just get that straight. I was defending myself. Every single time. Even with the gum. Felicia was a little bitch. She'd swirl around in her desk chair and smart off at me about my mom leaving me with the help. I didn't know what the hell she was talking about and it never occurred to me to wonder how she knew my mother left me.

Strawbridge is a small city. A backward, tight-assed hornet's nest is what it is. Everybody into everybody else's business. And these fancy, snooty types who act like they're all that will take every opportunity to remind you of it. Mel would tell me, "Big fish in little ponds," and roll her eyes. I get it now.

Anyway, so I put gum in her hair. And then I put gum in her friend's hair—Caroline Simmons, boy did she deserve it.

It didn't stop the torment. I was put in the back of the room at a table by myself so that Felicia and Caroline could pester me without me being able to do a damn thing about it. And when they'd get their goons to bother me on the playground, I tackled them and hit them. The shoe incident, well, that might be sort of my fault. Tenth grade. Strawbridge High. This cheerleader bitch. She turned to me in line at the cafeteria and sneered. "Nice shoes." Then she turned back to her little clique of snots and they laughed and laughed. I was wearing army boots, okay? So what? So...I stomped on her toes. Exposed toes. Dainty, painted toenail toes, sticking out for all the world to see in her strappy flat sandals. I might have broken one of her toes. I wasn't expelled for some reason. But I got to sit in the dean's office for a week writing essays. It was totally worth it.

The point is, Nicky and I crossed paths a lot. I'd be going into the principal's office, and he'd be coming out. I'd be pulled off some stupid girl while across the playground, he was punching a kid in the face. It's a wonder it took until last year for us to get together. I was a junior and he was out of school by then. He still hung out at the park down the way with Zeke who lived a few streets over. They'd go to the park to smoke weed and throw knives in the dirt and make their big plans. Nicky and Zeke were going to get rich stealing from people. I don't know why, except that maybe I'm stupid, but I thought it was possible to do that. And I agreed to help them.

That first day, I'd left the house because Mel was on my case about the mess in my room. It was always something; it was as if I couldn't do anything right, even if I tried. So I walked out and down to the park. It was dusk and all the little kids were in getting their dinner. I thought I'd be alone, but was glad to see the guys there, sitting in the dirt near the swings. I walked right over and stood facing them.

Nicky said, "Well, look at you."

"What?" I said. I thought maybe I'd done something wrong or maybe I had a big stain on my pants.

"All grown up," he said.

"So are you." I hated it when older people tried to talk to me like I was a baby.

"But it seems all the sudden with you."

"I'm pretty sure we grew up at the same rate."

"Last time I saw you," he said, "you were out trick or treating in your little witch costume."

I rolled my eyes and took a seat in the dirt. "What did you do? Go off to college?"

Here they both laughed. It took me a little while—hanging out with the two of them at the park after dark a few times a week—to realize they had a code. I'd say or do something that would make Zeke whisper, "Hold on there." And Nicky would say, "Holding strong." Over Christmas break, all three of us were walking through the neighborhood in the dark, the boys talking about robbing this house or that, and I tripped over something in the road and fell into Nicky. And Zeke whispered, "Hold on there." Nicky let go of me and said, "Holding strong."

I said, "Why do you keep saying that?"

They didn't respond.

"Tell me," I insisted.

"Jail bait," Zeke said.

Our first job was this house across town. It was in a richer neighborhood than mine but still not mansions or anything. No fences. No security. Zeke had been staking out the area and he said these people were out of town. So, Nicky shimmied open the sliding glass door in the back one night, about two in the morning, and we went in and found jewelry, laptops, an iPad, some game consoles. All sorts of stuff. We didn't take the TVs because they were too big. We had these big canvas bags, with pull strings at one end, and we loaded them up, stealing towels to wrap around the delicates, and left, pretty as you please. It was so easy. Too easy. And I loved it. I loved stepping over that threshold into the quiet, dark house. The silence pounded in my ears. It was as if reality shifted and it didn't come back to normal until I was outside again. Everything in that house was alien. In the kitchen, magnets littered the refrigerator; I took one—a cat, so far as I could tell in the darkness—and slid it into my pocket. I went into the bedrooms and stared down at the made beds, peered at the posters on the wall, looked into the closets at the kids' clothes. I ran my fingers along the sleeve of a hoodie. I was standing in someone else's reality, someone else's life, and I liked it.

Later, after I left Zeke and Nicky in the park going through the stuff, I slipped back into my house and into my room. I took the magnet out of my pocket and put it on my desk. I couldn't wait to see it in the light, to see what it was I'd really taken. And when I found it there the next day I rubbed it in my palms and held it to my lips. I had a piece of those other people now. I thought—I really think I believed it—that I could somehow absorb some goodness out of them through that magnet. But, of course, after a month or so it was hidden under other stuff on my desk, and I lost track of it for the longest time. I'd found no goodness in it, after all. Instead, it reflected the worst parts of me.

I went out almost every weekend with them, breaking into houses, taking little things: a three-inch wooden statue of a horse; a pair of bright pink shoelaces; a packet of *pot-pourri*; a tiny ceramic box with a hinged lid. The thing I regret taking most is a teddy bear. It was only about the size of my palm. But it was on a sewing desk. The next morning, I saw that a section of one ear was ripped. Someone was going to repair it. It must have been special. It took me about a month before I couldn't stand it anymore and walked all the way across town, one afternoon, to shove it in the owner's mailbox. I'm pretty sure I had the right house. I still feel bad about the whole thing.

And then I got caught. I was sneaking back in through my bedroom window when the light went on. Mel found me with somebody's tiny ceramic poodle.

"Where did you get it?" she scolded.

"It's mine," I lied.

"Where did you get it?"

"Nowhere."

That's when she started rummaging through the piles on my desk and gathering up foreign objects from the book-case. She accused me outright of stealing it all. And the next day, she marched me over to Mrs. Hawn's and offered me up as a servant. Nicky was thrilled. He'd tried to get into Mrs. Hawn's through her back door once and couldn't. And now I had a proper invitation. I didn't know it at the time, of course, but soon, he'd need money more than ever.

"There's got to be all kinds of stuff in there," he said when we met up at the park down the way that first night. "We could sell it."

"Yeah," I told him, "but it's buried."

"So dig it out."

How lucky was I that Mrs. Hawn wanted me to do that very thing? I like to think now that I wouldn't have stolen anything if Nicky hadn't got arrested. I like to think that.

28.

The idea to go to my mother's house hadn't actually occurred to me until Mrs. Hawn offered me money. Mel had asked me, "Should I tell her that I told you?" And I said no. Because my plan was to hurt her with it. To surprise her with it. My first thought was to write my mother a long letter. The first draft was angry and cruel. By the fourth draft, I'd come to understand something about the situation, I think. I'd started to imagine someone raping and beating my mother. Mel said he'd done that—split her lip, broke a rib. Then he forced her to walk home with him following her. Mel told me she'd thought about not going home, so he wouldn't know where she lived, but she didn't know what else to do. When she got to the driveway, he kissed her and wiped hair out of her face. He told her not to walk the neighborhood alone so late at night anymore. And if she told on him, he'd come back and kill her. So my fourth draft was kinder, more understanding. I was ready to forgive her.

But I never got the letter sent. It wasn't right somehow. The words felt false. I was trying too hard. It wasn't what was really going on inside me, somehow. Calling her was out of the question. Her voice on the phone, every time I'd heard it, was always distant—hard and cold. If I heard it like that, I wouldn't be able to say anything. And email was just rude, not that I had her email address.

When Mrs. Hawn wanted me to find her letter, I knew I was going to go across the state and see my mother. I was going to have to face her. And I had this idea in my head that when I did, she'd cry and apologize and then everything would be better. I didn't imagine she'd want me. I'm not that stupid. It would just be better. We could talk. Maybe be friends.

So I asked Nicky to take me there. I didn't tell him about the money—that I could pay for the gas and any food we'd need. We'd just left a house on Maple, in the neighborhood north of ours. He had a computer under his arm and Zeke had a bag of jewelry and a laptop.

"What do you want to see her for?" he wanted to know.

"I have to tell her it's okay."

"How the hell is it okay?"

"Quiet," Zeke said.

"She's still my mother."

"The hell she is. Look, if she couldn't handle it, she should have let you be adopted—let you have parents that loved you."

"She gave me to Mel."

"She did not."

"Damnit all," Zeke said.

"She did so," I whispered.

"She left you. Your gram had no choice but to take you. And you know it. She don't deserve forgiveness. I won't be a part of it."

I didn't get the chance to talk him into it. We heard a car behind us. Zeke said run. So I ran. Next thing I know, Zeke's sister came over while Mel was at work to tell me they'd been arrested. Nicky told the cops that I had nothing to do with the robbery—that I'd met up with them that night after it was done. Nicky's not so bad. Still, the police called Mel. She was supposed to talk to me about the company I keep. She went and told them I had stuff in my room that didn't belong to me. We had to gather it all up and take it to the police station. All the while, Mel was crying and asking, "Are you sure he gave this to you? You didn't steal it yourself?"

"The cop told you what Nicky said. I didn't have any part of it."

She believed me.

Nicky wrote to me while he was in jail. He still had hidden codes. He wrote, "How's the old lady you're work-ing for? Did she give you anything nice lately?" I wrote him back but never mentioned Mrs. Hawn. It's not like I liked her or anything, but maybe I did. It was just that going around at night with Nicky, sneaking into those houses, taking stuff—I didn't ever really think of it as stealing so much as hanging out with Nicky. That's what he wanted to do, so that's what I did. I didn't know what I planned on doing with my life, but I knew I didn't want to steal stuff for a living. And I didn't want to be in jail

By that time, anyway, I was thinking about the money. I could take a bus, I figured. I could find a way. And then the way landed in my lap. I didn't mean to lie about my mother. I thought the story I told was better than the truth, that's all. So I rode over there with Mrs. Hawn, all the time thinking what I was going to say to her. *It must have been awful. I under-stand. I forgive you.* But when my mother opened the front door and looked at me, then turned to glimpse back in the house and slide her way outside, hiding, like I was a dirty secret, it all changed. She ushered me out onto the driveway, farther from her family. Her family.

And she said, "What are you doing here, Hannah?" I could hear all of it in the way she said my name. Hannah, who's not supposed to be here. Hannah, who isn't part of my family. Hannah, who I don't love. Who I never loved.

Every kind thing I wanted to say drained away. "Mel told me." I glared at her, could feel my upper lip lifting into a sneer.

"Told you what?" She was nervous—afraid.

"Who my father is."

She reached out to touch me, but as she did it, she turned back to the house. She didn't want her family to see it.

"I came here to forgive you," I said. "I came here to tell you I understand and it's okay."

"I don't need forgiveness."

"Good. Because you're not going to get it."

She rolled her eyes. "Make up your mind."

"I think I have. I think I figured it out."

"Oh, really? What have you figured out?" Another glance at the house.

"If you didn't want me, you would have given me away, or had an abortion. And if you didn't care about me, you wouldn't have beat Trevor up when you saw what he was making me do."

Her eyes were concentrated on me then, her brow furrowed.

"It turns out I was right all along, wasn't I? You didn't leave me with Mel because you were raped. You left me because Gary didn't want me."

"You don't understand how it is."

"I think I do."

"For God's sake, Hannah. I don't have time for this."

"You don't have time for me. Of course you don't."

"I can't believe you came all this way to say that." She turned back to the house.

"Me either," I said. As I made my way back to Mrs. Hawn, something went wrong.

29.

When I turned away from my mother, I was angry. I thought I'd conquered something—proved something. But with every step I took toward the car, that all drained away and once I was sitting next to Mrs. Hawn, I found it hard to breathe. I struggled to keep tears away. I was hollow, except for the ache in the pit of me, and confused. I listened to Mrs. Hawn talking—forced myself to pay attention, else I was sure I'd drown in whatever was wrong with me. I couldn't look at it just then.

And everything happened so fast when we got back home. Mel and I turned at the same time, to find Mrs. Hawn lying on her driveway by the car. She'd fainted but was awake seconds after Mel got to her. I was sent for water and when I got back outside with a glass, Mrs. Hawn was sitting up, leaning against the car, trembling. We helped her into our house and she didn't make a fuss at all. I ran to plump up the pillows and turn down the bed in the spare bedroom and we sat the old lady down on the edge of the mattress, took off her shoes, and helped her lie back.

"I'm okay now," she said. "Just couldn't stand for some reason. Maybe all that time in the car."

"You fainted," Mel told her.

"Did I?" She looked at us, worry on her face, and then around the room.

Mel had done the room up nice. All in pale blue. A quilted bedspread. Two of those pillows that are only for show. Drapes at the one window that she made herself on the little sewing machine she has in the dining room. In one corner, she'd tucked a plump, soft chair. A round, wood table perched next to it on one side and a bookcase filled with books stood on the other. I used to believe she made the room for my mother, for if she ever came home. But just then I realized how useless the whole room was. What had it been sitting unused for all those years?

"A person could get lost in here," Mrs. Hawn said. And weirdly enough, I understood.

There was no time for me to talk to Mel, to tell her what happened. She called Mrs. Hawn's doctor and then we took her in. The waiting room was eerily quiet. No one else was there. Mrs. Hawn sat between us, each hand grasping one of ours. It felt strangely normal. I stayed behind when Mel helped her to the examination room and she didn't come back for the longest time. When she did, Mrs. Hawn was with her. Everything was arranged, Mel said, on the way home. Mrs. Hawn would be staying with us. Mel would be taking her to the hospital for more tests. I'd be with her during the day. And later, once we had Mrs. Hawn squared away in the spare room with a light meal, she sat down across from me at the little kitchen table and told me about hospice.

It reminded me of Allison Dorry. Death, I mean. Her mother died when we were in fifth grade. I remember all the whispering when she was absent for a week—it could've been longer. Even the teachers would gather in little pockets and shake their heads. When she finally came back to class, everyone acted as if she had a disease. Like death was catching and if they got too near, their mothers would disappear. But my mother was already gone. One day out at recess when everyone else was playing on the tarmac, I found Allison on the wooden steps of the P.E. portable. She had her arms folded across her knees and her chin resting on them. I stood there, sweating, in the sun, waiting for some kind of sign that I could talk.

"Go away," she said without looking up.

Allison didn't get better. It seems like everybody stood on the outer edges of her life, watching her self-destruct. What do I know, though, right? Maybe her dad put her in therapy. Maybe he did what he could do. But in the end, Allison Dorry disappeared. Literally. She went from this normal, almost invisible little kid, to a wild, addicted dropout, to a missing person. When news hit the school last year that she'd run away, or been abducted, or who knows what, I remember walking around for a long time feeling cheated. I wanted it to have been me. I wanted to disappear. And I hated it that I knew why I didn't. I hated that there was always this little kernel of hope in me that my mother would come back and get me. If she were dead, I wouldn't have to live with that. Allison Dorry didn't understand how lucky she was.

"We need to make her as comfortable as possible," Mel told me.

I nodded. "I'll have to keep feeding the cats."

"We'll get the keys from her."

There was more to do, of course. I had to find that letter. Mrs. Hawn told me to forget it, said it wasn't really important. But I knew it was. I thought about telling Mel. I imagined how it would go. I'd tell her I needed to throw away a lot of Mrs. Hawn's stuff to find it and she'd say I had to ask permission. I knew the old lady wouldn't let me do it. I'd probably tell her, once again, that she was dying, on her way out; what did she need all that stuff for? And then Mel would be horrified and make me apologize and then she'd accuse me of upsetting Mrs. Hawn, which she'd just told me not to do.

"How long does she have left?" I asked.

Mel looked at me as if I'd asked her if I could eat a bug. "Don't be morbid."

"But the doctor must have told her, and you were there."

"You shouldn't worry about that."

"Again?" I said, angry.

"Again what?"

"You're trying to protect me by not telling me the truth. Like you didn't tell me the truth about my father. I don't need protecting. And it doesn't work, anyway. It only makes things worse."

She took in a deep breath and laced her fingers together on the tabletop. Letting the air out in a grasp for courage, she said, "A month. Maybe."

I had to work fast.

30.

I had to set the alarm as quietly as possible to keep from waking Mel or Mrs. Hawn. It took me a few seconds to remember what was going on and when I did, I bolted upright in bed, reached over and turned the switch to stop the music playing. Then I sat in the dark listening...waiting to see if it worked. When I was sure they were still asleep—it was four a.m.—I got up, pulled my jeans and t-shirt on, shuffled into my sneakers and snuck out my window with Mrs. Hawn's keys. Inside her house, I'd piled eight large black trash bags filled with junk on her sofa where she always sat watching her little television. Two bags crowded the entrance to the hall. And the last two I'd left just inside the door, in the kitchen. I pulled them out first, then got the others and piled them all outside the back door.

The neighborhood was quiet. It reminded me of the nights I'd go out with Nicky and Zeke, when it seemed like we were the only people left in the world. Our voices, even when we whispered, echoed all around us. And now, the scraping of plastic against my legs as I hauled each bag around front and down the street lined with trash cans, waiting for pickup, roared in my ears like a jet. I was sure somebody would open a door and yell at me. I lifted the lid on Mrs. Harlstein's thick plastic bin and nearly choked on the stench. Rotten food and cat urine. Turning my head away, I lifted the two bags I'd brought, one by one, and set them on top of the others already inside and lowered the lid slowly, trying not to make a sound. I went back and forth, hauling trash bags down the street, depositing them into the neighbors' bins. After that, I set to work on the newspapers and magazines—they were much harder to deal with. There was no room in the house to make a pile ahead of time, so I grabbed armfuls and dumped them into the recycle bins, by that time gasping for air like I'd run a few miles. I kept telling myself that this was garbage. Mrs. Hawn wouldn't miss any of it. I was careful, even though I worked fast, to only get rid of trash. Real trash. I checked each piece of paper to make sure it wasn't important and flipped through the magazines, shook out the newspapers, in case she'd tucked something in them. One bag was filled with nothing but other plastic bags. I found empty soup cans, flattened frozen meal boxes—stacks of them—a large paper grocery bag full of cat hair and twisty ties. Mrs. Hawn had saved boxes inside boxes and shoes without soles and empty spray bottles. She had fourteen of those cylindrical CD holders, empty, in a pile underneath a rotted out quilt. Who would want any of that? I felt like I'd thrown away a truckload of junk, but I knew, come daylight, the house wouldn't look all that different.

I managed to get back home by six-thirty, just before Mel woke up and started her coffee. My heart pounded in my chest as I lay in bed waiting to hear the first of the trucks—trash or recycle—thunder down the street. I heard a quiet knock at my door and it made me jump. Mel pushed it open and peered at me in the early morning light.

"You awake?" she asked.

"Yes."

She came in with her coffee mug and sat on the bed

next to me. "It's been a busy few days."

I rubbed my eyes, trying to pretend I'd just woken up.

"We haven't really had the chance to talk about your trip."

"My trip?"

"To Tampa. With Mrs. Hawn."

I turned to the window as I heard the first truck. My stomach rolled a bit.

"I wish you would have told me what you were planning," Mel was saying. "I suppose I can understand why you didn't. Looking back on it, I can say I'd let you go. Of course. I'd have driven you over myself and not bothered Mrs. Hawn."

I heard the tinny clang of metal and glass in the distance. Recycle truck. I put my hand to my forehead, feeling a headache twisting at my brain between my eyes.

"But I guess I have to admit that's only hindsight. You're right. I wouldn't have let you go. I'd have told you to call or...something. Or asked you to just forget it. That's what I'd have done."

I shook my head and swallowed. The truck moved along the road, its two-pronged claw reaching out from its middle, squeezing each large bin, lifting it, and dumping its contents into the open top. Then it lowered the bins, and dropped them back onto the roadside. One by one. Down the street. Closer and closer. Until it was at our house. And gone. Only to make its way back, doing the same on the other side.

"I'm sorry about that, Hannah. Are you listening to me?"

I dropped my hand from my head and looked at Mel.

"I'm sorry I made you feel you couldn't trust me," she said. "I've been...well, I've been straddling the fence, that's what I've been doing."

"The fence?" I whispered. The truck was making its way

back to us. Half of Mrs. Hawn's trash was gone and there was nothing I could do about it. Even if I ran out now and tried to retrieve the bags I'd dropped in cans on the other side of the street, I'd already thrown away some of her stuff. It was done.

"I've been trying to protect both of you. Your mother. And you. I was wrong."

"Wrong?" I felt sick to my stomach then and my head pounded. I was scared thinking what would happen to Mrs. Hawn if she knew what I'd done. But it was too late now. She was going to have to accept it.

"When I didn't tell you about your father. I convinced myself I was protecting you, but I wasn't really. I could have told you when you were fifteen, maybe earlier. You've always been wise for your age. You had to be, I guess."

"What are you saying?" I realized that what I'd done was wrong. Mrs. Hawn was dying. It was like I only just then understood it. Dying. And in her final days, I'd betrayed her. What kind of person does that?

"I should have been on your side. Yours only."

"I understand."

"Do you?"

I sat up, scooting myself back against my pillows. "Yes. She's your daughter. Mothers protect their children."

We sat there for a few awkward seconds staring at each other. And I imagine we were both thinking it. Good mothers protect their children. But they're not all good.

"I've done something bad," I told her.

Mel reached out and put her palm to my cheek, smiling. "You can tell me," she said. "I'll help make it right."

31.

I was surprised that Mel's solution was to keep it secret. I told her about the letter. I told her about Oliver, and even about Mrs. Hawn's family—the ones who invited her for Thanksgiving. She said I should keep taking out the trash. Mrs. Hawn wasn't likely to get to go home before she died—she would never have to know. But, she said, if I found the letter, and if Mrs. Hawn asked me directly, I should be honest, tell the truth, and accept the consequences. That didn't feel right to me, considering the consequences would be upsetting a dying old woman. But Mel said that in almost all circumstances, the truth was more important, for everybody.

Then I heard her in Mrs. Hawn's room, asking her about her family. Was there anybody she should call? And Mrs. Hawn told her to mind her own business.

We moved the cats over to our house and that made Mrs. Hawn happy enough. But as the days passed, she started asking me for things.

"Could you go over to my house," she'd say, "and bring me my little table lamp. The one that sits next to my spot on the sofa?"

I brought over her little television set, the table it sat on, books, magazines—she never asked for specific issues so she never knew I'd thrown any away—some dolls, little figurines of cats and owls, and the sofa pillows. The spare room was starting to look like it belonged to somebody. We set her little figurines on the window sill so she could see them as she sat up in bed. She spent most of her time in bed. She watched television all day, all sorts. She read with it on, said she was multi-tasking, then laughed. I found a big plastic bag of yarn in the front room of her house and went searching for knitting needles. I couldn't find anything, but I took her the yarn anyway. She asked if Mel didn't have crochet hooks. I said, sure she did. And Mel and I went to the store that evening when she got home from work. We got a whole set of hooks and a few pattern books and stood at the door, watching Mrs. Hawn's face sink into something like happy reverie as she sat up in the bed, her hook weaving in and around the strand of yarn, one of the cats curled up against her leg.

The Saturday I got the letter from Nicky—the one that gave me the idea—I knocked once at her door and opened it to find her standing hunched over at the foot of the bed, her left hand touching it, and her other hand reaching out to the easy chair. She shuffled a step forward as I came in.

"Honestly," she said as she eased herself into it, "I can't tell if I'm weak, or if I'm just scared there's so much room to move around in."

I tried not to laugh. "I came to see if you're ready for lunch."

"That'd be real nice."

I fixed her up a turkey sandwich with some chips and a Diet Coke. She loved Diet Coke. I put a banana and a package of those orange peanut butter crackers she liked with it and took it to her on a tray. I put it on the little table next to her chair.

"So much food." She always said that.

"Some for later," I said. "I won't be back for a while."

"Where do you disappear to all day?"

"What do you mean?" Of course, I knew what she meant. I was over at her house, throwing stuff away.

"You're not hanging out with that boy again, are you? What did you say his name was?"

"Nicky. No. I told you; he's in jail."

She peered at me, her mouth pursed into a kiss, like she didn't believe me. "You deserve better than that."

I wanted to ask, "How would you know?" but I didn't. I nodded and sighed.

"So, where do you go?"

"Out," I said.

She rolled her eyes and slapped her hands against her thighs. "Fine. Don't tell me. It ain't like I give a damn."

"I'm at your house, okay?" I'm not sure what it was that made me say it. But I think, when I look back on it, Mrs. Hawn knew all along. She was just trying to give me the chance to tell her. And it exasperated her every time I came and went without owning up to it. "I'm looking for the letter."

Her face eased up, but she didn't smile. "You don't have to do that."

"I want to."

She turned to the window, let her eyes follow the top rim of the curtains that hung there, then turned back to me. "Thank you."

It was later that I got the mail and saw the envelope from the jail over in Sharpes. I'd just come from Mrs. Hawn's and was dusty and sweaty. I wanted to take a shower, but Mel had a rule about that. She said I'd take three showers a day if she let me. So, I changed clothes and sat up on my bed and opened it up.

"Dear Hannah," it read. "Why don't you write me back? I don't really have much to do here but think about getting out. You'll be older by then. Are you still helping the old lady? Find anything interesting in her mess? Write to me and tell me all about it. I miss you. I really like you, you know? I didn't want you to know before. Because, well, you know why. But I do. I won't tell anybody about what happened. I promise I won't ever do that. I'm probably not going to be in more than a year. I'd like to know if you're going to be there when I get out. Will you?"

I folded the letter up and slid it back into the envelope. This would be the third letter I got that I ignored. I don't know why I stopped writing back. Mrs. Hawn would say I do know, but I'm making myself look away from it. I thought about what he must feel like, him sitting alone day after day, waiting for a letter. And getting nothing. That's why I did it, I guess. And like Mel said, the truth is more important.

32.

Paige Hawn wasn't anything like her half-sister. She was trim and posh—wore pale pink polish on her fingernails. Her teeth were too straight and white, like fake teeth, but her smile was a bit crooked so it all worked out into a kind face, the sort you'd trust. I met her at the convenience store about a block south of the neighborhood, on Palm Cove Road—the two-lane stretch where it connects to U.S. 1—the section that a lot of people forget exists. It's old Strawbridge, maybe the earliest part, where everything looks decayed and warped in time. Paige pulled up in some kind of SUV, a dark, bloody red. The window slid down and she lifted big, white-rimmed sunglasses from her face and said, "Are you Hannah?"

I was going to roll my eyes. I was thinking, who else? But then I remembered where I was. I could have been one of the hookers or junkies, hanging out, waiting. Anyway, I nodded and approached the car.

"Hop in," she said. "I saw a Wendy's on the way over. We can get a soda and talk there."

Usually, it's not a good idea to get in a car at the convenience store. And I could feel the cashier's eyes peering at us from inside the store. I kind of liked the ideas he must have had rushing around in his head about me. He knew me well enough—didn't like me. He was sure Nicky and I stole candy bars and chips from him. We did.

Paige chatted as she drove back down Palm Cove, to where it became a four-lane, major road...into civilization, really.

"I was so surprised when you called," she said. That extra word 'so.' I don't know, there was something cheerleader about it. I tried not to like this woman, but it was hard to do. "You have no idea. I've tried to keep in touch with Lennie, but she's so stubborn, always was, I think. She moved out of the house after she graduated. Got a job, lived on her own, supported herself. We've tried to help but, frankly, she never needed us. I don't think she gets how much David and I looked up to her. I mean, sure, over the years Mom told us what happened to her. The bad things, you know? But that only made us admire her more. She always seemed so strong."

She bought us both French fries and Diet Cokes at Wendy's and we sat in a hard plastic booth at a window. She wore dark pink lipstick, it matched her jacket—one of those tweed things with all sorts of colored lines running up and down and side to side. It was fitted and I could see the pink satin lining peeking out from under the sleeve hem every now and then. She must have come from work—an office job. She was used to air conditioning. Why else would anyone wear a tweed jacket and matching skirt in the summer? I felt inadequate in my tank top and shorts, flip flops at my feet. No polish anywhere.

"You're staring," she said and shoved a French fry in her mouth. She smiled while she chewed.

"When did you see her last?" I asked.

She shook her head and sipped some Diet Coke through the straw, then patted her lips with a napkin. "Long time now. Five years, maybe. She came up for Dad's funeral."

"Have you seen her house?"

She took some time, wiping her hands off, folding and refolding her napkin, setting it back onto her lap under the table. Then she looked at me. "No. But I know what happened to her mother. And Mom told me Lennie had that problem. Is it bad?"

I nodded.

"I'm glad she's not still in it," she said. "I can't imagine what it must mean for you and your grandmother to take her in like this."

"I don't think Mel even thought twice about it."

"Which tells me it's really bad."

"It smells bad. There's a lot of dust. She couldn't wash anything, not clothes, not dishes." I watched her. She was nodding. "I don't think you'll really understand until you see it."

She sighed. "I'm prepared. You wanted to talk first. Why?"

"Honest?" I said. "I wanted to make sure you were nice. I didn't want you to see her if I thought it would upset her. It still probably will, you know. She doesn't want any family around."

"I can't imagine why."

"I can."

"Well, can you explain it to me? I mean, sure, I get that David and I were her father's second family. But she never hated us. She was only ever nice to us. I don't know why she stopped wanting to see us."

I took a few fries and shoved them into my mouth.

"Is she embarrassed?" she asked.

After a few sips of soda, I leaned in. "Sort of. But not about the house. It's more like...it's that nice people, well, people who love you, and see good in you—and you don't. I mean...it's hard when you don't think much of yourself, to be around people who can't seem to see that. It's like, you don't understand her, because you like her so much. Does that make sense?"

"Not at all."

I was looking at her face and I could see Mrs. Hawn in it. In the eyes, at the corners. And in the shape of the mouth. "If you could, when you see her," I said. "Don't tell her how great she is, or was."

"I can't tell her how much she meant to me...when I was a kid?"

"I don't mean that. You can tell her what you think, or feel. The problem is when people try to tell a person she's wrong about herself. Like, if she were to say she was a terrible big sister. You don't say, no you weren't. You say, it didn't feel that way to me. You get what I'm saying? Telling a person she's not the way she feels she is, well, it's like telling her she's a liar."

"I don't think I can agree with that." She looked even more like Mrs. Hawn when she said that. "If a person says she's stupid, you don't agree with her."

"But you don't tell her she's wrong, either."

"Why not?"

"Because it doesn't help. Don't you see? If I say I'm a liar and a cheat and you shouldn't trust me, you don't say, 'you are not.' Because then I think you don't hear me. I'm not really saying I'm a liar and a cheat."

"You're not?"

"No."

"Then what are you saying?"

"I'm saying I feel like I am and it hurts and I don't want to be, but I don't know how not to be. It's like everything I do just makes me more and more a liar and a cheat and I can't stop it. I don't want to feel this way, but I do and I just want people to hear me and...I don't know...understand."

Paige wasn't smiling anymore. She tilted her head to one side, her brows drawn in. She reached across the table and

174

let her fingertips rest on mine. It was like being touched by a young Mrs. Hawn. "I think I get it," she said.

33.

Paige visited with Mrs. Hawn for a long time. When she was finished, she came over to the house. I could hear her muffled hello, and then a cough.

"I'm back here," I called from the back bedroom.

I tried to imagine her picking her way through the maze in her tweed suit and lipstick, trying not to touch anything. But when I looked up to see her at the doorway to Mrs. Hawn's bedroom, I saw she'd taken off her jacket. She leaned on the door frame—not seeming to care about her silk blouse getting dirty—and looked around. She was horrified, sure, but she was no fussy whiner. I liked that about her.

"Are you cleaning stuff out?"

I was going through papers, checking for the letter, and throwing them into a large plastic trash bag. "She doesn't know I'm throwing stuff away," I said.

"Why are you doing it?"

"I have to."

"Can't you wait? It's awful to say," she said. "But once she's gone, we'll hire a company."

"But what about pictures and personal stuff?"

"They can look for that. There are businesses that do it for you. Specialists."

I nodded. "Well, I'm looking for something. Something she wants *now*."

"In this mess?"

I shrugged.

"How can you even be sure it's in here?"

"Well, I don't think she's thrown anything away in...like, ever."

I could see the hint of a sigh in her. I couldn't blame her. Mrs. Hawn was just somebody she used to know—like a long lost relative who you'd like to help out, but then again, maybe it's too much.

"What is it she wants?" she asked.

I kept shuffling through trash—magazines, boxes, kitchen utensils, old shoes—tossing it into the bag. "Did you know Oliver?"

"Oliver Stanton?"

"She knew him a long time ago, I guess."

"I know who you mean. The Stantons lived a few doors down when we were at the old house. Oliver was her age."

"There's an envelope or a letter. To Oliver. It sounds important."

"Well, I think they dated for a while. I didn't know there was anything more than that. Did she say anything about it?"

"Only that she wants it."

She looked around the room for a bit. "An envelope?"

"I know it sounds impossible..."

"No, I get it. I do."

I looked away—started going through trash again. I couldn't cry about it. Crying would only blur my vision and I'd miss the letter. "I have to do this for her. This one last thing."

"Okay," she said.

"Okay, what?"

"I'll be back. Do you need anything? To help with the

178

search, I mean."

"More trash bags."

Paige came back about an hour later with trash bags, thick gloves, and masks to put over our mouths and noses. She said, who knew what we'd be breathing in. She insisted I wear the gloves.

"I've seen those shows," she said. "God only knows what sharp thing is hiding in here."

She worked with me all that afternoon and came back that Saturday, too. Best of all, she put bags of trash in her SUV and took them to the dump herself.

I went in to see Mrs. Hawn later that day. She looked tired, small, scrunched up against the pillows in bed, half sitting, half lying down. Darwin, the brown one, curled up against her at her hip and she was staring out the window, even when she knew I was standing there.

"Are you mad at me?" I asked her.

She shook her head. "Why would I be?"

"For not telling you about Paige. Same as lying, I guess."

She looked at me then. "No. I'm a little mad about the trip, though. That was a really big lie."

It was about three days after we brought Mrs. Hawn to live with us that I knew Mel had told her the real story about my mother. We were sitting across from each other at the little kitchen table eating dinner—roast chicken and mashed potatoes. I'd been careful to put the chicken in on time and cut up the potatoes like she'd asked, but she still seemed angry with me. Usually, she started talking as soon as we sat down to eat but that night, she was quiet. Maybe it was Mrs. Hawn, I thought. But that hadn't stopped her from chatting the past day or so. After a while, when we were almost finished, I felt like she was waiting for me to say something. And then I knew she was waiting for the truth.

"I lied to her," I said. "She wouldn't have driven me over there otherwise. It's my fault."

She looked up, chewing, nodding.

"I told her I hadn't seen Casey since I was little. Told her you wouldn't let me."

"I know."

"She told you?"

"She did."

And all this time since that conversation, I hadn't said anything to Mrs. Hawn. I suppose I wanted it to just go away.

"I'm sorry about that," I told her later.

She was lying in the bed, her graying hair undone and spread on the pillow behind her head.

"Did Mel tell you *why* I wanted to see my mom again?"

"She said it was private—something only you could share."

I went to the window and looked out on the little back yard. The fence was covered with vines and two branches of Mr. Hurt's oak tree crossed over into our yard. I could hear Mel's voice in my head. "Shade is shade," she always said. "Whoever gives it."

"I've done a lot of bad things," I said. I turned back to her, surprised to see her eyes closed, her face pinched. "Are you okay?"

She swallowed hard and nodded, as if in her sleep. "I'll be fine, in the end. Don't you worry. Let me ask you though..." She opened her eyes and pushed herself up to sitting a bit. "You think I should go to Paige's?"

"Did she ask you to?"

"That she did."

"Do you want to go?"

"Yes. But only because I can't stand the idea of dying here, in this bed, with you just a room away."

I moved over to the bed and sat on the edge of it, twisting toward her. I reached out and pet Darwin's tail. "I can't imagine it," I said. "I can't think that one day you won't be alive anymore. I don't understand how it works."

"What do you mean? It's pretty clear. You live, you die."

I shook my head. "I understand it that way. But I don't, at the same time. I don't know where you'll be if you aren't...there."

"I won't be anywhere."

"You don't believe in life after death? In heaven?"

She chuckled and laid her head back against the pillow. "That doesn't make a whole lot of sense to me."

"But just not being here does?"

She closed her eyes again and smiled. "It scares you?"

"A little," I said.

"It scares the hell out of you."

I didn't respond.

"It scares us all. I ain't gonna—" she stopped, opened her eyes and lifted her head. "I'm not going to tell you I'm not scared. But I think about life like a circle. What I am is no different from what the dirt is, what the sea is, what the earth is and all the other stuff in the universe. I'm part of it now. I was a part of it before I was conceived. And I'll be a part of it when this body is gone."

"But you...your mind. Your thoughts."

"All part of it."

"It's not the same." I could feel something tugging at me, something painful, frightening, and I wanted to turn away from it.

"No," she said. "It's not the same. And that's what makes it good. But you see that fear? In your eyes, what's making your lip tremble?" She leaned over and put her hand on Darwin, too. "That's what makes me want to go to Paige's."

I had to get up and leave before I cried. I don't think it was because I didn't want her to know—she knew already. It was something else, something worse. It was just what I was telling Paige about earlier. I couldn't stand her caring about me. I want to say that I wasn't worth it, but that's not it. It was that I was afraid I was.

34.

The hospice nurses were at our house more and more and Mrs. Hawn was fading away. With Paige's help, I'd cleaned out the back bedroom, but I didn't find a letter to Oliver. After enduring a few days of them showing up without her permission, Mrs. Hawn started acting like she was glad to see Paige and David—he brought flowers every time. One Saturday, I heard them all in the bedroom laughing. It was good that Mrs. Hawn could laugh. She had some memories, at least, that were good. Maybe at the end, I thought—hoped—all the bad is forgotten.

One day—I think it was a Tuesday—I stopped in to see her before going next door. I had an idea that the letter wasn't in her bedroom after all. I thought it was in the front room, where she spent all of her time. She found it, I imagined, before the bedroom filled up and she put it in her pocket—the pocket of that house dress she always wore. And later, maybe one day when she got dressed to go to the store, she found it and set it aside...and forgot.

When I peered into the spare bedroom that had become Mrs. Hawn's home, one of the nurses was sitting in the chair by the bed, his hand on Mrs. Hawn's. They were both smiling.

"I'll leave you to talk," he said.

I stood in the doorway after he left.

"Well," she said. "What is it?"

She'd startled me and I could see in her eyes that she was glad. There was always something challenging in the old woman. She reminded me of one of my math teachers, Mr. Kenecky, who liked to bark out questions, to make sure we were awake.

"I know you want to tell me," she said. "Let's out with it."

I shook my head, slightly, barely visible but I know she saw it. Mrs. Hawn saw everything. I walked over and sat in the hard chair the nurse left by the bed. "I did something bad."

"We all have."

"This is really bad. I don't know if I should tell or not."

"You mean tell Mel?"

"Or the police."

"Ah, I see. Very bad." Her voice quavered, a bit, and I couldn't tell if it was the dying...the slow decay of it, or if she was thinking about something in her own life.

I nodded.

"You can tell me."

I sighed and looked across the room, out the window. Outside the world was baking. The end of August. Summer was red hot and threatening to stay until Christmas. The sand on the beach was too hot to walk on; enclosed garages were ovens; and there was no solace even in the shade. It was as if the air around us balked at summer's end, would have none of it, and so leeched every bit of heat from the rest of the planet and concentrated it right here in Central Florida. But I shivered.

School would start again soon—my last year. I'd have to decide about college, the future. Mel had already been nagging at me. We could afford it, she said, if I wanted to go away for school. But I didn't have to go away, she was quick to add. I could stay right here, go to the community college and then over to Orlando. But I was stuck and I wasn't sure how to get unstuck.

"About me and my mom," I mumbled. "The truth."

"Don't blame Mel. I told her what we'd done and why. She felt she ought to correct the story. For my sake."

"It's okay. But my dad..."

She waited. Patient. Like she knew I had something stuck in my throat and if she'd just stay quiet long enough, I could get it out.

"My dad was a rapist."

When you say something like that out loud, for the first time, it hurts. And I could see that Mrs. Hawn understood that. She didn't gasp, or shrink from me. Instead, her chin rose, just a little, defiantly. For me, I think. To give me power of a sort.

"Anyway," I said, "so you know I *did* get to see my mom...more than I admitted to. Still not a lot. She'd say it's my fault. What happened was, well, when I was thirteen, I went over there to spend the summer. I thought it was because they wanted me there. I thought I was going to stay. Nobody said so; I don't want you thinking they lied to me or anything. It was all in my head. So, over those few weeks, I don't know why, but I got madder and madder every day. It made me sick. Physically, I mean. I couldn't eat. I was vomiting. And Casey, that's my mom, she thought I was sick, you know? I told her I wasn't, so she accused me of being pregnant. I started throwing things."

"Did you know why you were sick?"

"Not really. Looking back, I can see I was jealous. I've got three half-brothers and a half-sister. When I was thirteen it was only three kids, and Casey was pregnant. Anyway, this one day, she went out, probably to the doctor. It was the day after she said I must be pregnant. I went into her room. I think I was going to steal money or jewelry. But I ended up looking at these pictures she had on her dresser. They were set in these really pretty frames. Gold and silver vines, hearts. They were all pictures of her and him and their kids. Their dog, too. I just...freaked out."

"What did you do?" Her tone was kind, not ominous or threatening, like she understood—like she'd have done it, too.

"I broke them all. The glass. I ripped up the pictures. I was bleeding. I must have gone into the kitchen for scissors, because I remember seeing blood dripping onto the counter top and I don't think I dreamed it. I dumped all of their clothes from the drawers—pulled them all off the hangers in the closet. I cut everything up. Even the pillows. Then I packed up, made myself some food to take with me, and left. Walked down the road, out of the neighborhood. I remember asking someone on the main road where the bus station was. They didn't know. They let me use their phone to call Mel to come get me."

"You got into some trouble, I bet."

"And they wouldn't let me come back. I didn't think I wanted to go back. I thought I was showing her that I hated her. But now I think I was just doing that thing people do. You know, we try to make sure everybody sees us the way we see ourselves; we want them to agree with how worthless we think we are."

"Where'd you hear that?"

I shrugged. "I don't know. Psych class maybe. It makes sense."

"I don't think that's what you were doing at all."

"No?"

"No. I think you were...then, and probably every other time, all the things you probably did to your mother, bad things. You did plenty, right?"

"I guess."

"You were giving her a chance to prove to you that she loved you."

"Why would somebody do such awful things—"

"They weren't awful to begin with, I bet. They start out small. They just get bigger because she keeps failing the test. Don't cry."

"I can't help it."

"She's the one with the problem, Hannah. Not you."

I wiped off my face. Mrs. Hawn reached over to her night table and drew a few tissues from the box she had there and handed them to me. I wadded them up, rubbed my eyes and nose.

"But that's not the bad thing you did," she said. "The thing you came in here to tell me. Is it?"

I shook my head and let more tears fall.

35.

Sometimes, Nicky and I went off on our own, after we'd broke into a house, or maybe before, while Zeke was still planning it out. Zeke knew about it when we went ahead of him; Nicky would tell him how we got in and whether or not he'd left the door unlocked or a window open. Nicky and I would sit in the dark on the people's sofas; we'd ease back in their recliners; and sometimes, we'd get into their beds. Zeke didn't like it. He said we were supposed to leave the place clean—said the owners shouldn't even notice right away that anything was amiss. But Nicky and I liked to sit in the kitchens and smoke cigarettes, flicking ash into a bowl or a potted plant. He always took the butts, thinking the police might get our DNA from them.

The week before he got arrested, Nicky took me over to a house on the corner of Palm Cove Road and Cecil. It was a big house, facing the main road, instead of the smaller one Rocks covered the yard instead of grass and over the back fence—six feet tall—they had a pool, a lot of concrete and rocks, a hot tub, and a little patch of grass at the very back where they'd planted bushes. Wherever these people had gone off to, they took their dogs with them. Huge, empty bowls sat outside the sliding glass door that Nicky jimmied open. We slipped inside.

When you sneak into a house at night, it means nothing. The house is like a cave and all you see is the little spots illuminated by your penlight. It's as if the house isn't real at all. It's just pinpricks of light. You're not doing anything wrong. You can almost convince yourself that you're rescuing these things you steal. Taking them out of darkness, a form of nonexistence, and giving them life. But it's different when you go into someone's home during the daytime. There is something ominous about a dark house during the day, when the blinds are closed but sunlight peeks in around the edges. You get the idea that the house senses you inside it and it's uncertain—it wants company, but it knows you're not its people. Nicky and I felt brave that day. It coursed through us like energy. We were someplace we weren't supposed to be. And we'd got there right under the neighborhood's collective noses.

I can't remember how it happened, exactly. I know that I'd been trying all along. I'd stand very close to him, let my arm graze against his, make my fingers barely touch his. If we sat outside, at the park, I'd sometimes drop my head to his shoulder, complain of being tired, yawn. And Zeke would say, "Jail bait." Nicky stopped responding. Stopped scooting away. And that day, in the master bedroom, at the foot of that big bed, he was behind me as we stood looking around, and I turned to face him, up real close. We stood there like that in the darkness, but not so dark I couldn't see his eyes, his lips. He kissed me, hard, like he'd been waiting to do it forever. I pulled him to the bed and he was on top of me. I let out a moan and he stopped. He jumped off the bed like I'd bit him and left the room. I curled up for a little while, staring up at the ceiling, then around at the dressers, the paintings of flowers on the walls.

I was sitting up, at the foot of the bed, when he came

back into the room. He lit a cigarette and handed it to me, then lit one for himself.

"I'm sorry," he said.

"It's okay."

"Let's go."

"Go on; I'll be there in a sec."

He glared at me and I looked away. "Just come on."

"I said I'll be there in a minute."

He left the room again and I got up and went through the drawers in the mirrored dresser against the wall. I found some linen handkerchiefs and a few thin cotton camisoles with lace at the necklines. I made a little pile of them in the center of the bed and sitting next to it, on my knees, I used the cigarette to burn it all. Nicky came back in and grabbed up the bedspread, using it to snuff out the little bits of burning fabric. He took me by the arm and led me outside, where we snuck over the fence and headed home.

We were quiet for a long time, while we walked, and I thought he must think the worst. So, I said, "I didn't do that because of you. Because of us...what happened."

"Why'd you do it, then?" He was angry.

"I don't know."

"Yeah, you do."

I shrugged. "I get mad, that's all. Especially in the dark. Shining the flashlight on stuff. It's like another world, where people are happy."

"Aren't you happy?"

"Not yet."

"What will make you happy? It ain't ruining other people's stuff."

"I don't know if I can be happy. I don't have those pictures that everybody else has—moms and dads and kids. Smiling and stuff. I think you have to have that to be happy." We were quiet again, until I said, "I'm sorry about what happened. I mean, us. I know I'm jail bait."

"It ain't that."

"It's not?"

"No, not really. I mean, sure, if we did anything and your grandmother found out and didn't like it, I could get into a lot of trouble. But that's not it, so much."

"Well, what is it then?"

He didn't answer right away and I thought maybe he didn't really have an answer. But he said, "I just think...I think you deserve better than this."

It's funny that it never occurred to me that other people might feel like shit, too. "You mean better than you?"

"If I could get out of this, I'd be good. But this life..." He pulled another cigarette out of the pack he kept in his front pocket and lit it. "What I'm doing here. It's not right."

"You want to stop?"

He nodded.

"Then stop."

"I will," he said. "Soon I will. Maybe go to school or something. Something respectable."

But I could hear that doubt in his voice. I knew that doubt—it crept into everything you dreamed about because you knew, way down deep, that you weren't good enough.

36.

I told Mrs. Hawn about the fire and about the other stuff I'd done. She seemed so small and wilted, lying there on the bed.

"I'm sorry," I said.

"About what?"

"I shouldn't be bothering you."

"Why do you suppose you're telling me all this?"

I shrugged. "Don't know."

"Sure you do."

That sort of pissed me off. "Everybody says I know stuff and I don't." I felt bad as soon as the words were out. You don't yell at dying people. You just don't.

Instead of looking hurt, she smiled and closed her eyes, let them rest for a few seconds before she opened them again. Everything about her shouted that she was dying ...except her eyes. That made me mad, and I don't know why. She'd say I know but I don't want to look at it. But I swear I don't have any idea.

"We all know so much more than we want to look at."

See? She said that a lot there at the end.

"So, think about it. Look at it. Why are you telling me?"

"I don't know if I should tell," I said. "I should...

shouldn't I? I should go to the police. But you know, Nicky says he and Zeke won't tell. Nicky won't say anything about the fire because he doesn't want me to get into trouble. And Zeke won't ever say I was with them the other times, because he thinks he'll be in more trouble, for contributing to the delinquency of a minor. But, I stole all that stuff. And I burned that bed. I should tell, right?"

She let out a strained chuckle. "I don't think I'm the one to say."

"But you told me about Oliver. You were trying to tell him something, weren't you? And you wrote it in the letter."

"That's right."

I thought when I said that, she'd be upset with me, but nothing changed. She was tired and...content.

"So you wanted to tell," I said. "But you never did. I should tell, right?"

She shook her head, ever so slightly and turned her eyes to the window, looking out. "How do I know? If I told what I did, would my life have been better or worse? Look at it." She turned back to me. "Look at my life. If I told, I don't think it would have been any better."

"But what was it? What did you do?"

She closed her eyes and didn't open them and I couldn't tell if she'd fallen asleep or just wanted me to go away. I slipped quietly out of the room.

I found the letter a few days before Mrs. Hawn died in the spare room with the nurse at her side. It was in a box in the hallway, just outside the bedroom door. There all along, waiting for me to clean up the room and throw away all of Mrs. Hawn's magazines and newspapers and outdated bills. Dolls and doll clothes. Cat toys and ashtrays. Piles of moth eaten clothing, some of it new with the tags hanging off, other stuff moldy and wrinkled like it'd come from the thrift store and she'd wadded it up and tossed it at the ceiling fan just to see where it'd fall. I was looking, I realized, for some clue in the junk—an answer or a reason. Was she trying to tell us something? Was she making some kind of poetry? Was the hoard a puzzle or was it her way of puzzling something out?

When I found the folded pages, yellowed a bit from age and probably from being shoved in that little box with odd pieces of jewelry—earrings without mates, pendants missing their gems—I opened them up and saw her writing, careful and rounded at the edges. Dear Oliver, it said. I folded the letter up and my heart beat hard in my chest as I walked it over to Mel's. I pushed open the bedroom door and she looked at me and knew.

"Could you leave us alone?" she asked the nurse. He nodded and left, offering me a hopeful, but realistic smile that said, 'not long now.'

I sat beside her, on the edge of the bed, handed her the folded letter and watched as she opened it, took a look, her face filled with concern, and folded it back again.

"Is that not it? Is it the wrong one?"

"No, it's the right letter. I just...I could have sworn I put it in an envelope and addressed it. I can see myself pasting a stamp on it."

"Maybe you changed your mind and took it out again."

"Or maybe I dreamed it. Maybe I dreamed it so many times that I thought it was real. Did you read it?"

"Of course not. You want me to go, so you can read it in private?"

She nodded. So I left.

I expected to find it torn to pieces when I saw her again. I imagined myself on the floor of my room, taping it together, trying to figure out what secret it held. But I told myself I'd never do that. I waited the rest of that day, the nurse going in and out. I was scared that Mrs. Hawn was going to die. I didn't understand how it could be that one second a person is alive and breathing and thinking and remembering and the next she was...just not. I was afraid she'd be there in the house, but not in her body. She'd be trying to tell me something and I wouldn't be sure—always thinking I heard a whisper, turning, and seeing nothing. I knew I'd be looking for her for years to come.

Finally, when Mel got home from work and the nurse left, before the night nurse came over, I went into the spare room and found Mrs. Hawn sitting up a bit. She reached out a hand for me to come to her and I did, sitting on the bed beside her.

"It doesn't look as bad as it is, you know?"

I frowned.

"I want you to understand. It won't be long now. It's a struggle. To breathe."

"I know."

"No, I don't think you do, Hannah. I want you to be prepared. Soon," she said. Then she turned toward the table beside the bed. "The letter."

I took it, started to give it to her. "What are you going to do with it?" I asked. "Do you want me to find him? Send it to him?"

She pushed my hand away. "No. I want you to keep it. Read it if you want. When I'm gone. And then burn it. Okay?"

I shook my head. I didn't realize I was crying until it was too late and I couldn't hide the tears. "I don't want to read it. It wasn't for me."

"I need someone to know. You understand?"

I stood up. "Okay." I was lying and I knew it. I left the room, knowing I'd have to go back in—I'd have to promise her that I would read the letter. A mumbled 'okay' wasn't good enough. It wasn't fair, and I knew it. I'd told her what I needed somebody to know. I'd unburdened myself on a dying woman. I had to let her empty herself to me. And didn't I really want to know, anyway? It was just that...the thought of her being gone, and reading her words...I'd hear her voice. I'd remember her face. I'd think about that time we rode to Walmart for plastic bags and the long hours to Tampa and the lies I told her. I'd remember that I got to tell her the truth before she left. That was all that mattered, really. Being able to tell someone.

I did go back to her. But every time she asked me to do it, begging me—was she really, or was I imagining it?—I could only tear up and promise in a vague and frightened voice. So, she had no choice really. On the day she died, she told me her truth.

37.

There were days in the summer, Mrs. Hawn—Lenore—said, when her mother wouldn't get out of bed, not even to eat. She'd send her daughter out for groceries, for a new top or a book she'd seen in a catalog or read about. And she'd lie in the little oval she'd carved out for herself on her bed, surrounded by her stuff. During the school year, she'd manage to go to work regularly. Somehow, as the years pressed on, and the house grew more and more cramped with stacks of daily newspapers mostly, her mother got smaller and smaller, to fit. To let the hoard squeeze the life out of her. By the end, she was a sliver of a woman and criticized Lenore for being too big. Lenore would ignore her; she'd creep through the maze of junk to her own little spot on the sofa in the front room and know that she was just the right size. That made so much sense to me when she said it, breathless and weak. It was so important to be the right size. More than that, though, it was necessary for everything around me to fit me. I don't think I got that really, until after she died.

Anyway, she said that when she was in her senior year of high school, in February, she came home from school one day to find her mother curled up on the sofa...in Lenore's spot. She was drunk again. And she wouldn't get up.

"Nothing I did," Mrs. Hawn told me, "could make her get up. She hadn't worked in a year by then, and now she wouldn't even go to the store. She huddled there, curled up in my spot, waiting to die. And I hated her for it."

"I can understand that," I said.

"Do you?"

"You needed a mother."

"No," she said. "I hated her for the mess. For dragging me along with her. For taking my life away from me and then wanting to leave. I didn't need a mother. I needed my life back. I realized, looking at her one day a few months later, watching her lie there smoking cigarettes with an ashtray on her chest, her eyes on the television sitting atop a stack of books a few inches from her face—I realized that I couldn't have my life back as long as she was alive."

That's when it happened, she said. And she didn't remember if she made it happen, or if it was just one of those things. Her mother turned to her, and lifted herself off the sofa slightly. The ashtray toppled to the floor and her mother reached for it, losing the cigarette. She fell over, put her arms to the floor to stop her fall, and when she rolled off the sofa, her feet dragged with her the blanket that she'd had on her legs. And the blanket pulled the stacks of magazines she'd been looking at with it.

All in one slithering swoop, she said. Her mother was on the floor with trash on top of her, screaming about her cigarette.

"I stood there." Mrs. Hawn was frowning, her face pinched. "I watched her try to get up, pulling at the pile of newspapers on the far side of the sofa. They slid down over her, like a waterfall, wave after wave. And I remember thinking, 'I slept there. For years I'd slept there and those newspapers didn't fall.' They wanted to fall on my mother. They only waited for an invitation."

I wasn't sure what she was saying at that point. "What happened?"

"I moved closer, around the stacks, to see her. She was on her back, struggling, pulling newspapers off her face. One arm was wedged under the edge of the sofa, but the other was slapping at the newsprint. I was standing a few feet from her. I reached over to my left, to one of the stacks of boxes and papers and bags and I...I pushed it."

Her eyes were closed when she said it and then they flew open. She grabbed at my arm, like a weak kitten pawing for attention. I took her hand and squeezed it. She nodded.

"I killed her," she said and closed her eyes again. "I killed her."

We never told Mrs. Hawn that we'd thrown away most of her stuff. She died later that day, feeling, I hope, still secure. She'd told her truth anyway. Maybe the stuff wasn't so important after that. She died just before midnight and Mel came into my room to tell me. I called Paige.

Paige had a nice funeral for her half-sister, up in Sandy Point, about an hour north of us. It was at an old little Episcopalian Church. On the outside, it looked like a toy—like a white pointed box, but inside it was spacious and airy. I sat in the front row with Mel. Paige told us to sit there. But I felt eyes on me—strangers wondering who I was. I was surprised at the number of people there. I didn't think Mrs. Hawn had any friends, especially not in Sandy Point. Everything she'd told me about her life seemed so long ago. Mrs. Hawn, in the casket at the altar, looked sunken and small, not like herself at all. There was no defiance left in the face. I had this urge to step up to the casket and lift her chin, pull her lips into a wry smile. The preacher guy said some Bible stuff and then let Paige and David talk. They told stories about Mrs. Hawn. When she was left to watch over them one evening, she lit the grill out back so they could toast marshmallows. She taught them how to bundle up sheets and towels and pillows all around the dining room table and crawl underneath it and pretend it was a bunker and the apocalypse had arrived. The people in the church laughed and it echoed. Bounced off the walls. The preacher stood again at the little podium and it looked like he was going to cry.

"I remember Lenore," he said, "when she was yay high." He bent over slightly and put his hand out at about his hip. "She'd run up and down the aisle after service every Sunday. Until her brother Will was laid to rest. We didn't see Lenore after that day. We're happy to welcome her home."

Nobody talked about the day she slit her wrists in the bathtub. Nobody talked about the hoard. And the preacher closed the lid of the coffin. Eight strong men lifted it, and carried it down the aisle and out the door to the hearse. We all followed across town, real slow.

"Do you have your headlights on?" I asked Mel.

"I do. How'd you know about that?"

"We've watched the processions down U.S.1, remember?"

"I guess."

I couldn't believe she didn't remember. We'd be stopped at a light and policemen on motorcycles would ride up and block the intersection while slow-moving cars rambled past. And she'd explain to me, every single time I asked, what was going on. I never got it. I didn't understand death and the car ride. "Never thought I'd be in one," I said.

"Everybody's in one sooner or later."

After a moment, I said, "Thank you, Gram."

"For what? And did you just call me...Gram?"

I smiled, but looked away from her, out the window. It did feel odd saying it. I should have tried it out alone first. Sure, she was my grandmother. But she raised me. Mel wasn't right. Gram wasn't right. Hey You wasn't going to work.

"Hello," she sang. "What was the 'thank you' for?"

Sandy Point was an ugly little place, at least the part we were driving through. Boarded up houses. Dying trees entangled in the power lines. Pot holes. I was glad to turn away from it, back to Mel. "The thank you is for making me help Mrs. Hawn. And helping her. Bringing her to our house."

"Don't cry, hon," she said.

"It's a funeral. I'm supposed to cry."

The service at the cemetery was shorter. We all had to sit in folding chairs under a tent, and it was hot as hell. I watched the coffin, hovering over the hole and I knew how hot and stuffy it must have been inside. She'd like that. A lot. So, I wrapped my arms around myself and breathed in the muggy, Florida summer, let myself be bathed in the heat. When it was time to get up, I was stuck to the chair and enjoyed stripping myself off it. I turned to follow Mel out from under the tent when Paige took my arm. I looked at her, but she was looking at the crowd. I followed her gaze to a tall, slim man wearing a dark gray suit and black tie. His graying hair was thin around the edges of his round, lined face. He could have been Mrs. Hawn's age.

"Oliver," Paige whispered.

38.

I didn't want to go to the party after, but Mel insisted. I told her that I liked the way I saw Mrs. Hawn in my mind. She was tough, but not so tough. And she told me all the important stuff. It was as if I got the real Lenore, not the one that other people saw. And if I went to the party and listened to all of those people talk about her, the way they knew her, she'd be changed for me. I didn't want her to change. But Mel said, "What if you can tell them something about her that will make them happy?"

"Like what?"

She didn't have an answer. I figured all the people who knew her when she was younger would think the end part of Mrs. Hawn's life was rather sad. She spent all her time cooped up in her nest. I didn't want them to try to tell me that she was somehow better before—that she'd lost something.

We were able to find a spot at the curb in front of the house. Paige lived on the golf course up north of town. Her neighbors brought food to her house and greeted everybody like we were sad and needed to eat. Paige said things, like, "I wish I'd kept in better touch," and, "I'm so glad she wasn't alone at the end." There were whispers, of course. Any time anyone looked at me, it was with a sort of pleasant pity—but it was sweet and thankful, too. Still, it told me I was right. When they thought of Mrs. Hawn they felt sad for her. Paige answered questions about the hoard, about Mrs. Hawn's mother, and about that time when she was very young and tried to hurt herself. Paige would say, "That was so long ago. We should think of the happier times." And the women would make that tsk sound with their tongues, as if to say Mrs. Hawn had no happy times. I got the feeling they liked that. It somehow made them feel better about their own lives.

That struck me as odd. Seems to me when you think someone's wasted it, life is diminished all over. You look at yourself and think, *me too*. What have I done, anyway? I've lived and I'll die. I have a feeling Mrs. Hawn would say that's enough. These people didn't see her sitting in her spot on the sofa surrounded by her stuff. She was fine with it. She was living the way she wanted to live and it was enough for her.

I found out from David that Mrs. Hawn learned cosmetology. I said, "What kind of science is that?"

He laughed and said, "How ironic you should say that. It's cutting hair. She moved over to Orlando and worked in a salon while she put herself through school. She got a degree in biology and taught high school for almost thirty years."

"She taught high school biology?"

"She sure did."

"When did she move to Strawbridge?"

"Years ago. She taught at Strawbridge High School for a long time before retiring."

I was surprised. It was like hearing that your best friend was actually a spy or something. And it was just what I didn't want—this other level of Mrs. Hawn.

When I realized Oliver was at the party, I followed him

around, watching him. He had a wife—a prim, tiny little thing with gray hair perfectly folded into curls all over. She wore pink lipstick and nail polish. I knew her house would be empty and sanitary. Oliver left her with a small group of women and came to stand with me at the kitchen table. He took a baby carrot and ran it through the ranch dip. Before he put it in his mouth, he smiled at me.

"You lived next door," he said. Then he popped it in his mouth and chewed, watching me.

"You're Oliver."

He wiped his hand off on his fancy suit jacket and held it out to me. I took it. Instead of shaking it, he squeezed it, gently, like a hug. Oliver's eyes were deep blue, like a pretend lake—one you'd see in a fantasy movie, too perfect to be real.

"She had a good life," he said. It was almost a question.

"I heard she was a teacher. I didn't know that."

He nodded. His smile was weaker now and he took another carrot to hide it, I think. He chewed. Then he said, "I hear she turned out like her mother in the end."

It was then I realized Mel was right. These people only knew half of Mrs. Hawn. I only knew half. But there really wasn't anything I could tell them to help them know the part I knew. Because...maybe I only knew my way and they only knew their way. Maybe none of us knew her at all.

Mel was at my side, her hand on my arm. I introduced them and then she turned to me and said, hopeful, "Ready to go?"

We said our good-byes to Paige and David, knowing we'd see at least Paige once or twice as she dealt with Mrs. Hawn's house next door, and left. It was still sunny outside, but I liked it. I stood on the little front porch for a second or two, letting the heat penetrate and wash away the chill of Paige's air conditioning. Then I followed Mel to the car. When I got in, I hugged my baggy purse to my chest and asked her to wait.

"Don't start it yet."

She sat with her hand on the keys in the ignition, looking at me, a question on her face. I just wanted to soak it in. The heat. The suffocating heat. But then I realized there was more to it.

"Wait," I said again. "Wait."

I jumped out of the car and ran back to the house. I started to knock at the door, and then realized I didn't need to. I went in and found Oliver.

"Can I talk to you?"

He followed me outside, onto the little front porch. Mel was out of the car, but she didn't come over. She stood at the driver's side, watching us over the hood.

"She didn't turn out like her mother," I told Oliver. "Not at all. Her mother died when her brother did. She was nothing but a body, trying to find a way to let go of living. But Mrs. Hawn wasn't like that at all. She was trying to find a way to live. The hoard...it wasn't her tomb. It was her way of coping with what she'd done."

He stared at me for a few seconds until it was uncomfortable. "She told you," he said, finally.

I reached into my purse and pulled out the letter, still folded. "She wrote this a long time ago. I think she wanted you to have it, but in the end, she changed her mind. Not because she didn't want you to know. But because she didn't want to burden you."

His hand trembled when he took it from me. I knew I was right. It wasn't knowing that was the burden. It was not knowing.

"I read it," I said. "It's what she wanted to tell you a long time ago."

He held it in both hands, his thumbs caressing it.

"I'm not sure I believe it," I told him. "Not the way she tells it, anyway."

He looked at me, worry on his face.

"But it's the way she remembers it. And I guess that's what's important. You'll understand...when you read it."

"Thank you."

We stood there for a moment—both staring at the folded papers in his hand. Finally, he looked up again, out toward the lawn, to the sky, the sun. He was sweating, still wearing his suit jacket and tie; there was a trail of it trickling down the side of his face.

"She liked the heat." His voice quavered. "She liked August."

I nodded and turned to Mel, standing, waiting, so patiently.

"Well," I told him. "My mom's waiting."

I didn't even notice I'd said it until after he'd offered me a quick hug and I'd started across the lawn.

Epilogue

Hannah

My Dearest Meagan,

Enclosed, you'll find the kitty magnet that you have so adored all these years. I always thought that one day, I'd tell you about it. But that day never came. Ever since you got your own place, it's as if it's frowning at me, reminding me. I can't enjoy getting ice cream out of the freezer without it haranguing me. You never knew it meant something to me. It's just a refrigerator magnet, after all. It doesn't look suspicious—doesn't look like it's holding secrets. But it is. And I think you should know mine.

I stole it. I spent a few months as a teenager breaking into houses with a boy I liked, stealing things. One time, we didn't steal anything, but I lit a fire in one of the bedrooms. The boy put it out before any real damage was done.

The thing is, I never told the truth about what I've done, until now...to you. I told an old friend of mine most of it. I wanted to know if I should go the police and confess. She didn't have an answer for me. So I've lived with this secret my entire life and I've kept that magnet on the refrigerator to remind me of the person I was back then. I made sure not to be that person anymore.

But it's more than that. It's not enough to not be that person. I had to learn to live with what I'd done without letting it make me crazy. (Yes, I know that you think I'm crazy anyway, but you're supposed to feel that way.)

I don't want you to be ashamed of me, but I will understand if you are. I stole things from my friend—the one I sort of confessed to. Pieces of jewelry, a watch, some pewter figures, and a whole set of silver flatware in a fancy box. I gave it all to a friend of that boy I stole things with. She sold it all and sent him the money while he was in jail.

I'd like to say I did it because I worried about him and wanted to help him. But I really did it because I was afraid he was going to tell on me—tell the police that I stole things, too, and that I set a fire. After he wrote to tell me he got the money, he never wrote to me again and I never saw him after he got out. I didn't care...and that's how I know that I was only protecting myself.

So, when I found the magnet in my bedroom one day, I remembered. I remembered stealing it. And I remembered not wanting to give it back, and not wanting to be caught. And I wanted to keep remembering that selfishness, because I was afraid that if I forgot, I'd do something like that again.

When I married your dad and we moved away, I left it with Mel because I felt like I was really leaving that part of me behind and I didn't need reminding anymore.

But you fell in love with the kitty when you saw it. You wanted to take it home with you and Mel insisted that you have it. It stuck to our refrigerator in Thornton all those years, insisting that one day, I was going to have to tell you the truth.

I want you to have it now. I want you to keep it always

as a reminder that we all do things we're ashamed of. We all lie and cheat at least once in our lives. But that doesn't have to turn us into liars or cheaters. We can be better. We can always be better.

Love,
Mom

Books by Dianna Dann Narciso

Women's Fiction by Dianna Dann
Camelia
Always Magnolia
Bury Me

Fantasy by Dana Trantham
Children of Path: The Kell Stone Prophecy Book One
The Wretched: The Kell Stone Prophecy Book Two
Mark of the Faee: The Kell Stone Prophecy Book Three

The Kell Stone Prophecy: Complete Trilogy

Story Runners
Shards of Kholkari (2017)

Paranormal Humor by D.D. Charles
Zombie Revolution

Children's Fiction by Dana Trantham
Wayward Cat Finds a Home
Zombie Cats

For more, visit
waywardcatpublishing.com